Anthony Gilbert and The Murder Room

››› This title is part of The Murder Room, our series dedicated to making available out-of-print or hard-to-find titles by classic crime writers.

Crime fiction has always held up a mirror to society. The Victorians were fascinated by sensational murder and the emerging science of detection; now we are obsessed with the forensic detail of violent death. And no other genre has so captivated and enthralled readers.

Vast troves of classic crime writing have for a long time been unavailable to all but the most dedicated frequenters of second-hand bookshops. The advent of digital publishing means that we are now able to bring you the backlists of a huge range of titles by classic and contemporary crime writers, some of which have been out of print for decades.

From the genteel amateur private eyes of the Golden Age and the femmes fatales of pulp fiction, to the morally ambiguous hard-boiled detectives of mid twentieth-century America and their descendants who walk our twenty-first century streets, The Murder Room has it all. ›››

The Murder Room
Where Criminal Minds Meet

themurderroom.com

Anthony Gilbert (1899–1973)

Anthony Gilbert was the pen name of Lucy Beatrice Malleson. Born in London, she spent all her life there, and her affection for the city is clear from the strong sense of character and place in evidence in her work. She published 69 crime novels, 51 of which featured her best known character, Arthur Crook, a vulgar London lawyer totally (and deliberately) unlike the aristocratic detectives, such as Lord Peter Wimsey, who dominated the mystery field at the time. She also wrote more than 25 radio plays, which were broadcast in Great Britain and overseas. Her thriller *The Woman in Red* (1941) was broadcast in the United States by CBS and made into a film in 1945 under the title *My Name is Julia Ross*. She was an early member of the British Detection Club, which, along with Dorothy L. Sayers, she prevented from disintegrating during World War II. Malleson published her autobiography, *Three-a-Penny*, in 1940, and wrote numerous short stories, which were published in several anthologies and in such periodicals as *Ellery Queen's Mystery Magazine* and *The Saint*. The short story 'You Can't Hang Twice' received a Queens award in 1946. She never married, and evidence of her feminism is elegantly expressed in much of her work.

By Anthony Gilbert

Scott Egerton series

Tragedy at Freyne (1927)

The Murder of Mrs Davenport (1928)

Death at Four Corners (1929)

The Mystery of the Open Window (1929)

The Night of the Fog (1930)

The Body on the Beam (1932)

The Long Shadow (1932)

The Musical Comedy Crime (1933)

An Old Lady Dies (1934)

The Man Who Was Too Clever (1935)

Mr Crook Murder Mystery series

Murder by Experts (1936)

The Man Who Wasn't There (1937)

Murder Has No Tongue (1937)

Treason in My Breast (1938)

The Bell of Death (1939)

Dear Dead Woman (1940)
aka *Death Takes a Redhead*

The Vanishing Corpse (1941)
aka *She Vanished in the Dawn*

The Woman in Red (1941)
aka *The Mystery of the Woman in Red*

Death in the Blackout (1942)
aka *The Case of the Tea-Cosy's Aunt*

Something Nasty in the Woodshed (1942)
aka *Mystery in the Woodshed*

The Mouse Who Wouldn't Play Ball (1943)
aka *30 Days to Live*

He Came by Night (1944)
aka *Death at the Door*

The Scarlet Button (1944)
aka *Murder Is Cheap*

A Spy for Mr Crook (1944)

The Black Stage (1945)
aka *Murder Cheats the Bride*

Don't Open the Door (1945)
aka *Death Lifts the Latch*

Lift Up the Lid (1945)
aka *The Innocent Bottle*

The Spinster's Secret (1946)
aka *By Hook or by Crook*

Death in the Wrong Room (1947)

Die in the Dark (1947)
aka *The Missing Widow*

Death Knocks Three Times (1949)

Murder Comes Home (1950)

A Nice Cup of Tea (1950)
aka *The Wrong Body*

Lady-Killer (1951)
Miss Pinnegar Disappears (1952)
aka *A Case for Mr Crook*
Footsteps Behind Me (1953)
aka *Black Death*
Snake in the Grass (1954)
aka *Death Won't Wait*
Is She Dead Too? (1955)
aka *A Question of Murder*
And Death Came Too (1956)
Riddle of a Lady (1956)
Give Death a Name (1957)
Death Against the Clock (1958)
Death Takes a Wife (1959)
aka *Death Casts a Long Shadow*
Third Crime Lucky (1959)
aka *Prelude to Murder*
Out for the Kill (1960)
She Shall Die (1961)
aka *After the Verdict*
Uncertain Death (1961)
No Dust in the Attic (1962)
Ring for a Noose (1963)
The Fingerprint (1964)
The Voice (1964)
aka *Knock, Knock! Who's There?*
Passenger to Nowhere (1965)
The Looking Glass Murder (1966)
The Visitor (1967)
Night Encounter (1968)
aka *Murder Anonymous*
Missing from Her Home (1969)
Death Wears a Mask (1970)
aka *Mr Crook Lifts the Mask*
Murder is a Waiting Game (1972)
Tenant for the Tomb (1971)
A Nice Little Killing (1974)

Standalone Novels

The Case Against Andrew Fane (1931)
Death in Fancy Dress (1933)
The Man in Button Boots (1934)
Courtier to Death (1936)
aka *The Dover Train Mystery*
The Clock in the Hatbox (1939)

An Old Lady Dies

Anthony Gilbert

An Orion book

This edition published by
The Orion Publishing Group Ltd
Orion House
5 Upper St Martin's Lane
London WC2H 9EA

An Hachette UK company
A CIP catalogue record for this book is available from the British Library

ISBN 978 1 4719 1058 6

www.orionbooks.co.uk

To
Amy Shawe-Taylor
Affectionately

Contents

THE FAMILY

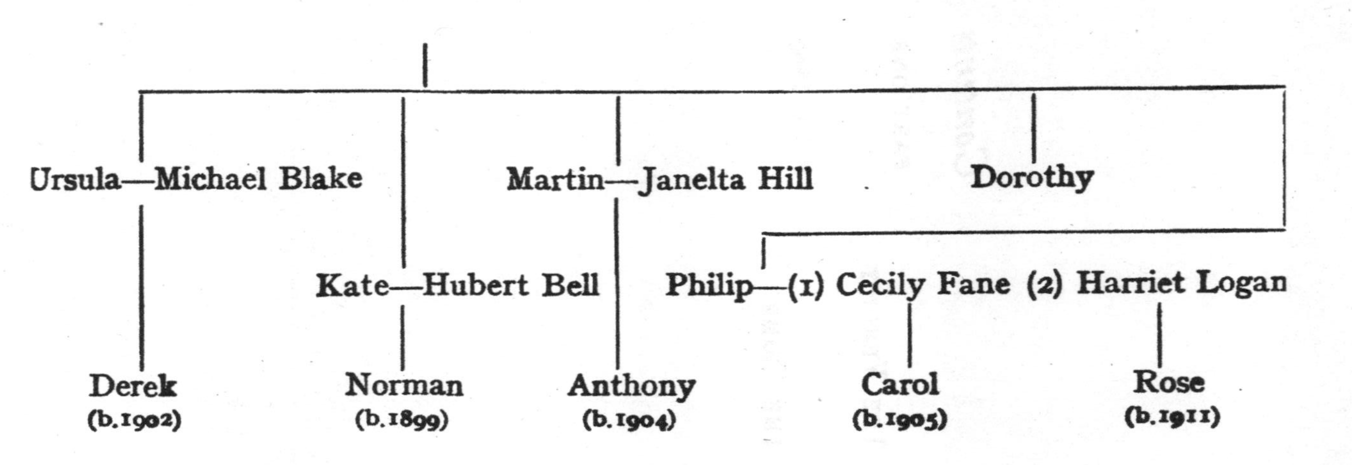

Bertha Harriet—(1) Michael John (2) Simon Wolfe (no issue)
Ursula—Michael Blake
Kate—Hubert Bell
Martin—Janelta Hill
Dorothy
Philip—(1) Cecily Fane (2) Harriet Logan
Derek (b. 1902)
Norman (b. 1899)
Anthony (b. 1904)
Carol (b. 1905)
Rose (b. 1911)

Part I
THE VERDICT

CHAPTER I

" NOBODY could call me a superstitious man," said the landlord of the Barleycorn, " but I say—and I'll say it again with my last breath—that the man or woman that laughs at gypsies is a fool. I know as well as every one else that they're a poaching, lying lot, as like as not, and I don't want 'em specially where I am. But if they was there I wouldn't be such a fool as to try and turn 'em away."

" Afraid of a knife in the ribs one dark night, Mr. Bowie ? " inquired a semi-facetious member of the audience.

" Knife nothing." Mr. Bowie was contemptuous. " No, but there's no blinking the fact they do know more than ordinary folk. See more, if you know what I mean. That's got nothing to do with brains. Most of them, I daresay, couldn't spell the word. But there's animals the same. You have a dog in a house that's supposed to be ghost-ridden, and that dog'll see things you'd hardly believe. But that's not brain. And I'd see the new moon through glass and sit down thirteen to a table before I'd turn any gypsy off my place. Look at that old woman up at the Hall, she had the gypsy's curse put upon her forty years ago now it must be, and it's powerful yet."

" That great red-faced old woman that goes about with a dumpy yellow-haired daughter ? " asked a newcomer, rattling his tankard ostentatiously.

"Mrs. Wolfe—that's her. Of course she was Mrs. John in those days, new married to Mr. Michael and proud of it. You wouldn't think it to see her now, simply waddling with fat, but she was a good-looking woman when she came here, big-made and dark with black snapping eyes. It was never hard to say who wore the breeches in that house, but Mr. Michael didn't seem to mind. He'd been easy-going from a boy. But there was a rare to-do when she found out the gypsies at the Queen's Paddock and said they'd got to go. Of course, in a manner of speaking, they were trespassing, but who'd ever given a thought to that? Gypsies there've been at the Paddock as many years as I've lived here and I was born in the place.

"'I won't have those thieving brutes on my land,' Mrs. Michael said to her husband. 'Poaching rabbits and stealing fruit. . . .'

"He tried to talk to her, but you might as well tell the rain to fall upwards instead of down. She hadn't got more sense than most Londoners; it was her husband's paddock, which meant it was hers, and she wasn't going to have any one so much as nibbling a blade. Of course, the Paddock isn't there any more now, since they started building over to Margetstown; land was worth a lot then and Mr. Michael had been dead for years, and his lady sold out. They say she's worth a mint of money, but she's welcome to it for all the fun it gives her. Just sits up in that great gloomy house with that daughter of hers—and no thanks to her that *she* isn't a madwoman too, the way her mother treats her—and counts what she's got."

" Go on about the gypsies," urged the newcomer.

" Oh, she had her way, of course. Went down to see them herself. ' Out you get,' she told them, ' or I'll have the police on you.' Never threaten gypsies with the police. I'd as soon put a live match by a Mills bomb and expect nothing to happen. They went, of course; gypsies like police about as much as rabbits like ferrets. But before they went the old woman—they said she was a hundred and I daresay it was true—she laid a curse on Mrs. Michael in life and in death, to have no joy in marriage or love in children, to live lonely and die of treachery. I wasn't there myself at the time, but I've met men that was, and they say it was enough to make the flesh creep on your bones to hear her."

" And it's come true ? "

" True enough so far. It was little joy she had in marriage. Not that I blame Mr. Michael or have anything against him. He was a good friend to me. I couldn't have bought in the nearby stabling and made this into a place where the gentry 'ud come and spend holidays for the fishing and so on but for him and the money he brought to the place. It wasn't only what he drank himself, though that was enough for three ordinary men ; it was the men who'd come from all round about to meet him. You couldn't forget him once you'd seen him. It was as if, after the curse, he changed, wasn't under her heel the same way. He got into a big roaring, swaggering fellow, standing over six foot, with a great mane of yellow hair and a laugh you could hear on Bull's Tor." Mr. Bowie was silent a moment, remembering the magnificence of those half-forgotten orgies, the dead man's huge shining face, with its sparkling eyes, the amazing, unforgettable stories he told, the sense of warmth and vitality he brought even into a half-chilled bar on the dreariest evening.

"And he's dead?" ventured the newcomer.

"Been dead these twenty years. Had a fit of sorts, and died with a strangling choke and a snore you could hear a quarter of a mile away. I saw him afterwards—there's a custom here that the village can see the gentleman at the Hall in his coffin, and for all the crazy woman his widow was she didn't dare go against that. He still looked ruddy and warm, as if he was remembering, and liked his own thoughts. But I'll never forget the look his widow gave him as he lay there, with those great hands of his crossed on his breast and some one had put a white rosebud in them. It seemed odd, that, a man like a bull and that little white rose. But all Mrs. Michael was thinking was of the bags of money, her money, mark you, she was burying with him, money he'd had of her and spent roistering and drinking and wenching. Oh, he was a proper man after the curse came on him. There's a story, but it's not for me to say how much truth there is in it, that he even took a stick to her once, and if he did, serve her right. She wasn't head in her own house in those days, which is one of the reasons, no doubt, that she took poor Ted Wolfe ten years afterwards."

"And he, is he dead, too?"

"Not he. She'll keep him alive the way a cat keeps a mouse, for the fun she gets out of him. Poor Ted. He didn't know what he was doing when he said Yes to her."

"He said . . . ?"

"Yes. Oh, she was like the grand ladies in history—leastways their gentlemen were. What they call *droit de seigneur*, which means you can have your pick of the village wenches and no one'll ask questions. Ted never thought about her like that. Well, why should he? He was just the fellow that brought her poultry and eggs and shook in his shoes when she complained. He wasn't doing too well, Ted wasn't; you know how it is with some men, doesn't seem to matter how hard they work, they can't make it. Parkinson now, that was in the same lay, anything he touched did fine. He was smelling out after the Hall custom, as Ted knew, and he'd take a penny off the price of fowls and a farthing off eggs, Ted would, because once he didn't go to the Hall any more he was finished. There was plenty of people who'd go to Parkinson readily enough. Not that he didn't work, too; he did, but that's how the luck was. Then one day Mrs. John sent for him; he says he hadn't a thought in his mind but that she had some complaint to make, but, instead of that, she said she'd been considering and she'd like him to marry her. Ted says he was stark, stammering, couldn't answer her. He wasn't above forty then and she must have been sixty if she was a day. She told him to come back next morning. Look at it how you would it meant ruin for him if he said No. You might ha' thought it meant ruin if he said Yes, but Ted had his feelings, and his farm meant a lot to him. He thought with a bit of money behind it he'd make it pay, branch out a bit. Besides, there'd be plenty of folk who'd come to him when they heard he was married to the lady at the Hall. Ted saw himself quite the gentleman farmer. And he didn't think she'd go on more than another ten years. He'd be no more than fifty then, and prosperous, and he could marry a girl to his own liking and breed up children. Oh, he had it all very pat. He'd been after two girls before that time, but one married a fellow from London and they've got six now in two rooms, by all accounts, and the other got into trouble with a gentleman down for a month's fishing. So Ted never had much luck. But he never did himself a worse turn than when he said he'd marry Mrs. John. To begin with, she wouldn't let him go ahead with the farm. She wasn't going to be a farmer's wife, she said; so Parkinson bought that in, and he'd send his hired man driving around in Ted's new milk float that had been the pride of his heart. As for Ted, he lounged around the house, afraid to give orders to the servants, terrified of his grand wife, knowing every one was making game of him. Having a rich wife wasn't any catch; he soon learned that. He'd expected to be able to dip a bit into what she had, but he soon found she kept it as tight as tight. I remember his coming in one evening—he used to sneak down here sometimes for a bit of a chat and p'raps a game of billiards—and telling me he didn't know how he was going to stand it. What did she want to marry me for? he asked. As if he never looked in his mirror! He was a good-looking chap, big and brown, with blue eyes and a lot of thick hair. But after his marriage he was nothing better than a slave. It wasn't just the farm. He hadn't been brought up the same way as her, and she didn't mean him to forget it. She was always bringing him up against something that 'ud make him feel strange and awkward. Even his clothes he wasn't allowed to choose for himself. She'd have none of his comfortable coats and breeches. He had to go to a tailor she chose for him, and when the bills came in she'd pretend to forget he'd had that suit, and she'd dress him down for extravagance."

"Not much of a man, is he, to let an old woman domineer him that way?" suggested one of the audience.

"You put yourself up against the woman he married and see what you'd make of it," the landlord adjured him grimly. "If she'd been a younger woman it might ha' been different. But she was always ailing, nothing bad but enough to have the doctor in and a general vexation, and the poor chap never knew what to do with himself."

"And she married him for his blue eyes?"

"Partly, I daresay. But she wanted something to kick, and she knew he'd not kick back. She's got that unmarried daughter of hers, the only one left of the five—that prophecy came true, too, as I'll tell you in a minute—but she hasn't got a kick in her, with her Yes, Mama, and Of course, Mama everywhere. Can't call her soul her own that girl can't. Oh, there was others 'ud have married Michael John's widow and welcome. There was the doctor, never had a penny in his pocket till that crazy sister of his died last year and left him £40,000 and the rector, that's a widower with two children to send to school. Either of 'em would have said Yes, but she couldn't have treated them the way she's treated Ted. She's got him down all right ; but she'd best be careful. One of these days she'll go a step too far even with him."

" Live lonely and die of treachery," murmured the visitor with a shudder. " Well, the first part's not true. She's got plenty of people up at the house."

" That don't stave off loneliness. I should think she's the most solitary soul in the place. No one's got a warm word for her, and all those that belong to her are just waiting for the day of her death."

" Are there many of them ? "

" Those I've told you of, and the grandchildren, five of them. Oh, she's rare mad she can't buy them with her money. A lovely lot, they are, all in London, not giving a damn for her. But the prophecy was true about her children. It's little enough joy she's got from them. One by one she lost them. There was Martin, the eldest son, that married a play-acting woman with the finest red hair I ever saw. His mother never forgave him, though Mrs. Martin could have given points to any woman in these parts. But Mrs. Wolfe thought it the Hand of the Almighty when the pair were killed in a railway accident when their boy was about sixteen. He's got her red hair, and he's on the stage, too. Anthony his name is. And both her daughters ran away from home, the first one, Miss Ursula, with a foreign music teacher, Italian or Spaniard or something, one of these tall dark chaps about as trustworthy as a leopard. I can still remember Mrs. Wolfe's face the day the news came in that the fellow had fascinated some other woman and left

Miss Ursula and her little boy, Derek, stranded in London. She looked as if she'd had a packet on the winner. That was the second marriage that didn't turn out right, to her way of thinking. And Miss Kate, the handsomest of them all, a big dark blooming girl, broke her engagement with Sir Robert Braye to marry some kind of doctor who died from taking poison. What they call research work. Miss Kate came back but her mother wouldn't have aught to do with her. You've made your bed, you can lie on it, she said, and let your son lie with you. That was Mr. Norman, that's a doctor himself now. The only marriage that did please her was Mr. Philip's. When the others had gone, she poured everything out on him. He was going to have the money and the place, if she could work it. He married a pretty pink-and-white bit his mother chose for him. It was the only family wedding they'd had. We all came to see it and the children threw rose-leaves. Then the next news was there was a girl, born on Christmas Eve, so they called her Carol ; and two or three years after that there was a boy ; but he died, and his mother with him within the week, and after that—not much more than a year after that—Mr. Philip married again. And this time it wasn't to please his mother. He married a woman on the music-halls, I believe ; Mrs. John, as she was still, cursed him, but she couldn't stop him. They lived in London after, and they had one daughter, too, that they called Rose. She doesn't come down here much, a saucy-looking girl with a mouth like a pillar-box and great dancing eyes. Writes the kind of thing you see in the Sunday papers. Where she gets it all from I don't pretend to guess, but if she was my gal, I'd have leathered her proper before she got to this pitch, writing on society vices and drugs and the misbehaviour of lords and ladies that, according to her, behave as my cows 'ud be ashamed. Put her in service, Mrs. John said. Learn her to keep a house nice. But lordy, I should think their kind of house would be more like a pig-pen than anything. Though I will say for her she looks smart enough, a bit too smart for me. Of course, Mrs. Wolfe hates 'em all, except Miss Carol. She says she's like her mother, though I don't see it. Taken up nursing, and whenever the old lady has one of her bad turns, down Miss Carol comes, and sooner or later down comes all the others. Likes to keep them on the run, Mrs. Wolfe does."

"I suppose, if she's rich, they daren't say No."

"Maybe that; though no one knows how the money'll be left. Close as an oyster she is. She's told Miss Carol she'll be the heiress, but that may be all bluff. No one even knows how much she's got. Runs into six figures I've heard people say; but that's just talk. We none of us know."

"Do they come down often?" asked the stranger.

"Every six or seven months she has an attack. Don't ask me of what. No one knows. So down comes Miss Carol and a few days later down come the rest. She hasn't died yet. . . ."

"She's to die by treachery," the stranger reminded him, and there was a sudden silence in the bar.

Then the landlord said, "They're down there now, came yesterday. Mr. Derek first; and then Mr.

Anthony, and then the other two together." He was silent a moment, then said, "They do say hereabouts that Miss Carol and Mr. Derek are going to make a match of it when he's any money."

"What's his job.?"

"He's not got one. He just writes books that folks seemingly don't want to read. They're none of them like their grandmother that could put any man right about the number of pence to the pound."

CHAPTER II

THE ritual of their grandmother's periodical indisposition was by now so uniform that whenever any of Carol John's cousins heard that she had been summoned to Aston Merry they automatically made their preparations for following in two or three days' time. On Thursday, the 20th October, the five cousins were celebrating Derek's thirty-first birthday at his club, that was both expensive and exclusive. No one pretended to know how he contrived to pay the subscription, any more than they knew how he met the fantastic rent of his rooms in the Adelphi—that, he said, he chose for the sake of atmosphere—considering his books generally sold something under a thousand copies, and he had no private means. Indeed, all his scapegrace Spanish father had left him was a handsome face and much charm of manner. Derek had added the anglicised edition of his name, not caring much for his Spanish inheritance.

After dinner a page came in to tell Carol she was wanted on the telephone.

" A case, I suppose," remarked Norman Bell professionally. He was the only really successful member of the five, a neurologist of some standing, though he was still only midway between thirty and forty. His detractors said he'd simply copied a famous and now titled physician who made his fortune telling patients he'd never seen any one so tired in his life. Norman told his rich spoilt neurotics, " Yes, marriage is a wearing business, I know," though, as a bachelor, as Anthony once pointed out, he couldn't conceivably know anything of the kind. To-night his thin distinctive face looked worn ; he had his ambitions like other men, and he sometimes agreed with his grandmother that it was a waste of life to minister to pampered women with nothing better to do than indulge in breakdowns. A few of his grandmother's thousands would make all the difference to his life. He'd be able to set up his clinic for the kind of people who really needed treatment.

" What's the odds it's grandmother ? " demanded auburn-haired Anthony cheerfully.

" Why should it be ? "

" Well, we've been talking about her half the evening. It would all fit together so nicely. I'm old-fashioned ; I like a pattern myself."

He laughed as he spoke, and Norman thought you'd never see Anthony fitting himself into any one else's pattern. He had enough vitality and imagination for six—Norman sometimes envied him there—and no amount of disappointment could really get him down. He'd say, being a true Anglo-Saxon he believed life was meant to be tough. And it probably was for him, with his fastidious tastes and his demands for perfection; though here again you had the paradox of a young man living from hand to mouth, buying his clothes in Savile Row and getting his shoes from Peal. Anthony said that clothes were the expression of the man, and to be badly dressed implied, with him, an inferiority complex. Though no one with a body like his need ever feel inferior, thought Norman, accustomed to bodies that had been abused and subjected to unnatural treatment. To see him stripped for running was to see a creature as beautiful as a boy on a Greek frieze.

Carol came back, her small head, with its cap of golden hair, smooth and lustrous as silk, rising from her barbaric gown. " Prepare to neglect your work next week," she greeted them. " Grandmother again. I ought to go now."

" You can't go down to-night," Derek protested.

" No, but there's a revolting train that leaves St. Pancras about eight o'clock in the morning. I must catch that, and there are a lot of things to see to before I go, and I shall have to pack. It's nearly half-past ten now. Thank you for my nice dinner, Derek. It's a pity you don't become thirty-one more often."

" I'll come with you," Rose offered. " I'm so good at packing that when Fleet Street rejects me I shall apply for a job as lady's-maid."

Anthony went to command a taxi from the gorgeous commissionaire, and the half-sisters departed.

" Poor Carol," said Derek. " What are you going to drink? She has the hell of a time with that old devil. She seems to think she owns Carol body and soul. Of course, Car's an angel to her."

"Oh, no," disagreed Norman. "Just a nurse, though I dare say the outward result's the same."

"I never saw anything quite so perfect as Carol to-night," mused Anthony, who set a very high value on what was beautiful and rare. "She makes me think of Perdita

"Each your doing
So singular in each particular
Crowns what you are doing in the present deeds,
That all your acts are queens.

By the way, what does grandmother think of cousins marrying?"

"She doesn't know, and she shan't if we can help it. If she'd never given the subject a thought before, she'd discover instantly she'd objected to it all her life."

"I don't see why she need find out at present, anyway."

"Unless Carol gives it away. She's so confoundedly honest. I've often thought George Washington must have been an embarrassment to his friends."

"You may be right. As a matter of fact, I'm much sorrier for her husband and Dorothy than I am for Carol. They have to be on the spot all the time. Honestly, I often wonder that there aren't more domestic murders. In Wolfe's place, I'm sure I should have brained grandmother with a hatchet years ago."

"She's his bread and butter, after all," observed

Norman unsentimentally. " And he's probably got used to living soft."

" They're an absorbing kind of household to any one with a speculative mind," suggested Anthony whose imagination, rich and penetrating, could cover a wide range. " I wonder some one like you, Derek, doesn't find any amount of material there. Grandmother, that indomitable tyrant, Dorothy, the woman of mystery. . . ."

" Mystery ? "

" Yes. Who's to know what she thinks, how she feels, what her secret life is ? She's an individual, but none of us has ever seen under the surface. It would be like groping your way through a new city. And that huge solitary house, and the three living practically isolated from their neighbours. For Uncle Wolfe's cut himself off from his friends by marrying into the wrong circle, and grandmother doesn't have much truck with the village these days. I wonder what sustains Dorothy. There must be something to keep her going, instead of collapsing with nerves, all these years. So the scene's all set for tragedy, which is your long suit."

Anthony went home alone presently, and Derek and his remaining cousin walked back to Cavendish Street, where Norman lived. On the way they discussed a new violinist whom a friend of Norman's had recently heard in Berlin, and whom he had described as a genius. The newcomer was to give a *premiere* English performance at the H—— Hall the following night, and Norman and Derek arranged to go together.

" Hayden's crazy over him," Norman said, fitting the key into his front door. " Says he's never heard such a violinist in his lifetime. You'll come in ? Oh, good. Lord, what a way to spend your time—making music. We'd better meet at the hall, I think. I have to be out to-morrow afternoon from half-past three onwards, and I may not be back till late. Leave my ticket at the booking-office, if I'm not there when it starts. Sorry I can't offer you anything to compete with that champagne of yours to-night. How the deuce do you run to wines like that ? "

" Ikey Mo," said Derek casually.

Norman looked startled. " Serious ? "

" Of course. Don't look so shocked. Have you never heard of Jews before ? "

" I've nothing against Jews," said Norman soberly. " They're among the few races in the world who'd support an artistic community solely on its merits. But Jews as artists are one thing, and quite another as moneylenders. I wish you'd come to me, Derek."

" Oh, I'm much too deeply dipped for that," said Derek, still without concern. " It's all right. Presently the wheel will come full circle, and I shall pay my rent and my tailor as regularly as any suburban householder. There's an ambition for you."

Then the telephone rang and an agitated voice asked if Norman could come at once. There'd been a bad smash.

" Curse them ! " said Norman dispassionately. " They go flying about at fifty miles an hour, and then expect a man who's already done his day's work to come round and patch them up."

" I thought you were a specialist," remarked Derek innocently.

" They don't draw the line even at specialists in emergencies," Norman assured him, without humour. He was moving about collecting what he'd need, instruments and drugs, leaving a scrawled message for his housekeeper in case of further calls. " All I hope is it isn't fatal. Doctors loathe inquests. It means wasting a whole day and not so much as your expenses paid. Mercenary, isn't it ? " He grinned and was gone.

CHAPTER III

I

THAT was Thursday night. The telegrams from Aston Merry came early on Tuesday morning. Derek, starting at once, caught a train by the skin of his teeth and reached Aston Merry in time for lunch. Carol, looking rather exhausted, came to meet him in the hall.

" How is she ? " asked Derek, kissing her regardless of possible eavesdroppers. " All right. I can see for myself. She's wearing you out. I suppose that's part of her fun. I wish to goodness she would peg out this time. I suppose there's no chance of it ? "

" She was bad yesterday ; she's better to-day. You never can tell with grandmother."

" I know. She's like these talented actresses who can weep to order. She throws a fit whenever she feels she isn't attracting enough attention. She must love to think she can drag us away from our work. I wonder really why we come. I suppose we don't see that you should have all the kicks."

"It's partly hysteria," Carol agreed; "but she's bad enough while it lasts. She's on morphia again. Dr. Marshall has just gone, and he's coming back to-night. Oh, here's Aunt Dorothy. She's been sitting with grandmother. Had Derek better come up, Aunt Dorothy?"

"Mama heard him. She said he was true to tradition, being first on the scene, but it wasn't much use the early bird getting up unless he was sure there'd be a worm for him."

"Grandmother's so cynical," Derek complained. "It never occurs to her that he might have thoughts above his stomach. The sunrise, for instance. . . . Heavens, here's Anthony. What train did *you* come by?"

"Oh, I jobbed a lift," said Anthony coolly. Just what you might have guessed, Derek thought. "I had a man I knew coming more or less this way, and I thought he might as well have a companion. What's the news, Car? I bet this is one more game to her. Our grandmother's staged as many farewells and come-backs as a fashionable prima donna. This is at least the fourth time we've been summoned down with hymn books in our hands and the price of a moderate wreath in our pockets."

Dorothy John was looking flustered and unhappy. She was a plump, pink, unpowdered woman in the middle forties, with yellow hair piled untidily on the top of her head, and a skirt that dragged over her heels. Her aim, thought Anthony critically, seemed to be to clutter up her appearance with as many frills, bows and furbelows as her rag-bag could assemble. She wore a belt with a brass buckle and used safety-pins galore, yet there was nearly always a hiatus between her old-fashioned high-necked blouse and her heavy skirt. She was always at a loss in an emergency, was unfailingly good-tempered and meek, swept ornaments off tables whenever she passed through a room, dropped trays at the invalid's bedside, and was as frightened of her mother now as when she had been a trembling child of eight, liable to drastic punishment.

" Oh, Anthony, dear," she expostulated. " Suppose grandmother were to hear. You don't understand. You're young. . . . You know, I do like that red hair, whatever Mama may say. Janet's was just the same. You're very like her, you know, though she wasn't a bit good-looking."

They all laughed at that, and at the sound a newcomer joined them from a small room on the right of the heavy front door. Ted Wolfe was a handsome, sullen man, grown a trifle stout now that he had adopted an inactive life, but his manner with his wife's grandchildren was always one of embarrassment. Dorothy, he could despise, a feckless body that had never had a man after her, but these youngsters were different. He said jerkily, " Oh, is that Norman ? No. 'Day, Derek. 'Day, Anthony. Happen you don't know if Norman's coming down ? "

" He's sure to, I should think. He'll come by road, though. D'you want to see him ? "

" Yes, I do. If he comes."

" He'll come all right. Blood's thicker than water. Though, really, a man as busy as he is might think twice, especially considering the way grandmother treated Aunt Kate."

Dorothy had turned and gone upstairs again. Carol said warningly, " You ought to be a bit more careful. Aunt Dorothy's quite likely, without any malice aforethought, to repeat all this conversation from sheer nervousness."

Wolfe surprised them by demanding with sudden passion, " D'ye think she's really like that ? I've sometimes thought no woman could be such a fool as she seems. It's a dark house here," he added abruptly. " You'll tell Norman when he comes ? "

" What's he got on his conscience ? " speculated Derek, watching the retreating figure.

" He's another mysterious soul for you. I wouldn't be a bit surprised myself to know he's got a sweetly pretty little thing somewhere in the village. Well, I'm sorry for him if grandmother ever finds out. And personally I wouldn't risk it, with a rich wife so near the Golden Gates as his is. Let's pay our respects to grandmother and then go and talk to the lunch."

II

Norman arrived in the early part of the evening, bringing Rose with him.

" I knew he'd be driving down," Rose explained calmly, " so I thought I might as well save my fare." She stood in the dark hall, a small confident figure, with a tiny scarlet beret jammed like a penny bun over one eye, and a flat red felt flower in her dark coat. She seemed to Anthony to bring the life and dazzle of London into this dim backwater. "Ought I to go and see grandmother? And how bad is she?"

"Norman's gone straight up. She's only seeing us one at a time to-day—Car, of course, not counting as one of us. You wouldn't like to take my bet that grandmother's got us on the hook once more?"

"No. I'm much too broke. I suppose there's no chance of touching her ladyship for anything? I do think she might have the decency to remember that people don't step in and pay your rent because your grandmother's gone all temperamental. Some of us have to work for a living."

Norman soon came back, and Rose disappeared. She was away about ten minutes, then they all heard the slam of a door and she flung into their midst, scarlet with rage.

"Has she disinherited you?" asked Anthony soothingly.

"Did you try to make a touch?" Derek suggested.

"Of course I didn't. Stones would weep blood before grandmother would cough up a sixpence. She'd want to know what the Poor Law Authorities existed for. Anyway, I shall never see a penny of her money."

"What happened?" asked Norman patiently.

"She's turned me out, neck and crop, with her curse upon me for ever. Quite in the style of the seduced daughter of Victorian fiction. If ever I have occasion to summon my relatives again, Carol," she imitated the old woman's voice to perfection, "kindly remember that this young person is nothing to me."

Norman said curtly, "She's a sick woman. Couldn't you have kept the peace for one night?" And he thought, "She wants slapping, and that's a fact. She may go down all right in Fleet Street, but she can be too much of a good thing down here."

"All very well for you to lecture," flamed Rose. "It wasn't you whose mother was insulted. Suppose she'd taunted you with having a mother who'd gone mad——?"

"Rose!" Even Anthony was shocked at that. He caught her by the wrist. "Don't be a damn fool."

Rose jerked herself free. "Shut up! Well? You see, you don't like it any better than I do, Norman. And you're not the only person with feelings. Though, of course, she wouldn't say that to you, because she knows it was her fault. But when she begins talking about Hattie as if she were some one who might be thankful to be made an honest woman of . . ."

"What are you talking about?" asked Derek.

"Grandmother. And Hattie. She meant to be insulting about Hattie. I saw that the minute I got in there. She began by asking very politely how she was. So I was just as polite and said she sent her respectful duty, and told her about a baby owl that Phyllosan, our bull-terrier-airedale, picked up in the next-door garden, and how Hattie goes the round of the mouse holes in flannel trousers and a jersey at unearthly hours, getting food for Athena. We've christened her after Florence Nightingale's owl, you see. It would make the R.S.P.C.A. quiver to hear her crooning. And then grandmother said what an entertaining mother I had, but she believed that was her profession before marriage. I said, Yes, she'd been an illusionist, and hadn't found it necessary to change it afterwards." Here Anthony chuckled, and the hand holding Derek's cigarette shook. "Well, that rather annoyed her, and she said I needn't speak of my father like that. He'd treated Hattie extremely well. Of course, that spilt all the beans. I asked her what the hell she meant, and she implied that if Hattie was lucky to be a wife, I was lucky to have a father to acknowledge me. The lousy old beast! So I told her what we thought about her and her money, and she told me to clear out, though not till the morning. There isn't a train up to-night, and she isn't going to be involved in the expense of a car. Her fine feelings don't run to that."

"You could hardly expect her to adopt an attitude of Christian meekness and offer to amend her ways," Anthony pointed out. "And this seems to me the only alternative."

"I expect it is," Rose agreed. "Anyway, it's better than this idea of turning the other cheek. I've never met any one myself who does that, and if I did I'd think them sanctimonious hypocrites."

She flung out of the room again and they heard her angry feet going up the stairs. Then Anthony said, "You know, I don't feel very safe indoors myself, with so much fur flying. Coming, Derek? It's a nice night." As they reached the hall, he added, "And that gives dear Uncle Wolfe his opportunity for a *tête-à-tête* with Norman."

CHAPTER IV

I

NORMAN did his best to avoid the interview. He haa nothing to say to his companion, and didn't want to be made the recipient of intimate family unpleasantness. But as he turned, with a cool word, towards the door, Wolfe said awkwardly, " Oh, Norman—just a minute. I wanted to ask you something."

Norman turned back courteously. " I'm for it," he thought with a groan. He recognised the expression on the older man's face. He was pretty desperate.

" It's quite simple," blundered Wolfe. " But—you're a doctor, aren't you ? "

Norman frowned. " If you want to consult me professionally, I'm afraid you can't," he said. " Unless, of course, you haven't a doctor of your own."

" I haven't, and that's the fact. There's no one but Marshall, and I don't want him running to my wife with everything I tell him. Oh, you think doctors don't, but you don't know my wife."

Norman said nothing. He looked thoughtfully at his companion, seeing a square, uneasy man, wearing expensive clothes in a manner that robbed them of all virtue, with hands and feet whose instincts were for handling machinery and tramping through meadows and lanes, not for remaining prim and inactive in drawing-rooms. He was a handsome fellow according to certain lights, with a high colour and blue eyes and a thatch of brown hair. No wonder people gossiped about the couple, thought Norman. Their dissimilarity was so obvious and embraced every department of life. Not socially, mentally or physically did they suit one another. Every one knew that and thought the position rash, disgusting or exciting according to their own temperaments.

Norman cursed his inefficiency at getting planted with the fellow, and wondered how soon he could extricate himself and rejoin his contemporaries. He took out his cigarette-case extracted a cigarette, lighted it, dropped the box of matches back into his pocket. The small sounds he made, the scrape of the lucifer, the rattle as the box fell, his own footsteps as he crossed to the fireplace and deposited the match in the coal-scuttle, all these were distinct against a background not of casual but of straining silence. Meanwhile Norman was confident in his view that Wolfe was going to be confidential, probably embarrassingly so.

" I cannot and will not listen to family confidences," he resolved, " it's an intolerable position." But, just as he was about to explain that he couldn't really be consulted in these intimate affairs, Wolfe broke in desperately.

" It's just this. D'you think you could give me something to make me sleep? I'll explain. I'm nearly crazy with—insomnia they call it, don't they? I shan't be able to stand much more of this. You don't know what the last year's been like.

You're only here for a night now and again. I'm never out of the place. Still, I haven't been like this before, tossing and turning the whole damned night. I know there are things fellows can take to help them. I thought you might be able to give me a prescription or something. After this evening's performance I really feel I'm at the end of my tether."

" A sleeping-draught, you mean ? Oh, that's simple enough. Couldn't you have asked your own doctor, days ago ? "

" There isn't any one here but Marshall and I don't want to have him rushing to my wife with his tongue out saying I'm asking for drugs. Next thing you'll have her accusing me of wanting to murder her. I tell you, Norman, she's as mad as a hatter sometimes. And if she heard me asking for veronal or chloral or whatever the best stuff is . . ."

" H'm," thought Norman, the professional in him rising immediately to the surface. " She would. Point is, would she be so far out ? And what's a fellow who says he knows nothing of sleeping-draughts doing being so glib with his veronal and chloral ? Why couldn't he have chosen bromide ? "

He began to talk without any change of expression, suggesting bromide or sulphonal tablets. Wolfe looked doubtful ; was Norman sure they'd do the trick ? He didn't mind what he had, so long as it was efficacious. His eyes roamed from one object to another as he spoke ; he never looked steadily at his companion.

" I want something that 'ud make me go off at once," he muttered uneasily. " None of these damned dreams, either. I tell you—if you're afraid of giving me veronal because it's a drug and you think I might get that I couldn't do without it and presently go off my head, I'll do that anyway pretty soon." As though he had taken some tremendous decision he suddenly flung down his defences, trampled on his diffidence, and made his companion a present of the position.

"Of course, this is in confidence," he said warningly. "It's not p'raps a nice thing to say, but if I can't get it off my chest somehow I'll go crackers. I can't help it that you're my wife's grandson. They tell me you're a very clever chap in London. And I've got to open up to some one."

"Oh yes?" said Norman tentatively. You might as well try to stop a runaway truck now as try to arrest Wolfe once he had made up his mind to unburden himself.

"I don't suppose you can imagine what it's like for my sort of fellow in a house like this. Of course, I'm not pretending that a lot of it isn't my own fault. I should have looked farther ahead, I expect, but could any man guess she—she'd treat me as she has? Good Lord, you don't know." He stopped and rubbed a handkerchief over his forehead. "They say you make the bed you have to lie on," he continued, "but there's many a bed looks easy and well-sprung enough till you come to stretch out on it, and then you find you can no more sleep there than you could in a nettle patch."

Norman headed him off as well as he could, but it was not easy. Wolfe had reached the stage where he must discuss his position with some one, for the mere satisfaction of sharing his distress. Norman listened with his usual patience to the wretched story of disappointment, misunderstanding and wilful humiliation. He didn't make any comment; he knew well enough that he could do nothing to ease the situation.

"Tell me," he said, "what's the crisis that started this sleeplessness? How long has it being going on?"

"Oh, about six weeks I should think. What started it? Well, money in a way. You might say its been money all along. I haven't any, of course, and I thought she was giving me a square deal when she said we'd both sign all the cheques. I didn't see how it was to work out. Of course, when she wanted my signature on any of her cheques, she just slapped them down in front of me and said, 'Put your name here.' I only once asked what she wanted the money for and, my word, she told me where I got off. I've never asked her anything since. You know," he moved with restless unease about the big florid room, "I never feel I'm safe. Any time she might decide to make me dependent on Dorothy or make some humiliating condition. One thing, she won't risk me spending her money on any other woman. And fifty's no age for a man to start again."

"But she's never said anything to give you that impression?"

"It isn't so much what she says. It's her looks and her voice. Dorothy knows as well as me. Of course, she may not get a stiver either. But if it goes to that girl, if you can call her a girl when she's not far short of my own age, I can whistle for my share. She'll jump at the chance of doing a bit of trampling. Oh, don't make any mistake. Let her loose and she'll plant those great flat feet of hers all over me."

Anger and fear combined were inducing a native vulgarity. Norman felt his reaction crystallising into dislike. He said shortly, "I doubt if any sedative will be much use to you, much lasting use, I mean. It's simply a case of mental disturbance. Unless you can make up your mind to stop worrying and take your chance, you'll go on lying awake of nights. As a matter of fact, I think all's well for the present. My grandmother seems to have made one of her spectacular recoveries."

There was, however, no answering gleam of relief on the troubled face of the man opposite him. Wolfe stood up, saying, with a curious roughness, "Ah, maybe. There's nothing sure, nothing clear. What did she want with me to begin with if she was going to treat me like dirt? Weren't there other men she could ha' bought, her own kind of men?" He stood by the table, a vein pulsing so fiercely in his forehead that he trembled from head to foot with suppressed emotion. Norman began to write a prescription on a slip of paper.

"This is for you to take to your chemist," he said, passing over the folded sheet. "Not that you really need a prescription. All these men keep sleeping-draughts and tablets for insomnia, but at least this one won't do you any harm, which is more than you can say of a good many mixtures."

Wolfe seemed to pull himself together; he took the bit of paper, saying with the bluff heartiness he supposed fitting among cultured men, " Ah, yes. Well, we'll see." Then his brow clouded again; clearly he was trying to key himself up to painful and stammering speech. " Happen you couldn't lend me twenty pounds just for a few days, Norman?" he broke out at last. "The fact is," his square, highly-coloured face took on the hue of a plum, " I've been betting a bit and I haven't been lucky. Seemed a sure thing, too."

" Does my grandmother object to betting?" asked Norman idly, feeling for his cheque book and reflecting that he might as well say good-bye to that twenty pounds for ever.

" She calls it lining others fellows' pockets with her money. Women don't seem to understand that you have to pay for companionship and a bit of fun the same as you do for anything else. She thinks if you can't bring the thing back with you and put it on one of the tables in the drawing-room it's money thrown away. Reckon she'd have had a bit more fun if she could ha' seen things straighter."

Norman passed the cheque across the table. " I think we might keep that transaction to ourselves," he observed amiably.

Wolfe took the cheque with an assumption of ease, looking uncomfortably grateful nevertheless. "Very good of you, I'm sure, my dear boy," he remarked in what he believed to be the tone commonly affected by men of Norman's world in such circumstances. " I'll give you an I.O.U."

Norman hastily stopped him. " Not a bit of it. You won't forget. That's all right."

"Well, it's all in the family," Wolfe agreed with another clumsy laugh and made his escape.

Norman was left to brood on the position; he wouldn't see that money again, but he didn't grudge it to the poor devil. Besides, even from his own point of view, it was money well laid out. He was a man perpetually interested in motive and reaction, and this intimate picture of a remarkable woman pleased his sense of the curious. Absently he folded up his cheque book and restored it to his pocket. As he did so the door opened and Anthony came in.

"Hallo!" he exclaimed, coming to lean against the table, the ash from his carefully polished small pipe sending a delicate shower over Norman's formal striped trousers. "Norman, what is this that I detect? You, our cautious cousin, parting to that red-necked scoundrel. Not blackmail, I hope."

"No," agreed Norman equably. "All the same, Tony, don't you marry a rich woman."

"None of them will look at me. And I can't afford to look at the poor ones."

"Well, you've time enough," Norman soothed him.

"You can't tell. I've just heard Car point out to Derek that all grandmother's children predeceased her, and I'm beginning to think we may follow their example. Except Dorothy, of course. Odd, how one keeps forgetting her."

"She won't wear Rose down," said Norman. "A young tank couldn't do that."

"I don't believe it would. She gets that from Hattie, not from Uncle Philip. I once asked Hattie what he was like. She said a nice little man with sleeked-back hair, and a bowler, and an attaché-case.

Doesn't that sum him up? He and Dorothy seem to have been the only two who didn't get any adventure out of life."

"Oh, I dare say he found Hattie adventurous enough. That marriage must have been very galling for grandmother."

"But very consoling to a low fellow like me, who might otherwise be utterly crushed by his refained relations. I'm all for Hattie myself. She's like a cabbage, a vulgar, hearty, beautiful cabbage."

"Are cabbages beautiful?" demurred Norman.

Anthony nodded with emphasis. "I once saw a shoal of them one early morning at Covent Garden, tight greenish-blue balls, with silver where the light touched them. With crisp curled leaves—I've never been able to eat a cabbage since, except at places like Derek's club, where they treat them with the artistry they deserve. I can't face the dishonour done to them by the unimaginative English cook. Hallo." He had strolled across to the window, whence could be seen the silver willows for which the house had once been famous. Years of wind and tempest had bowed them almost to the wall's level, but now as the breeze touched them, they shook out their silver banners with a rustle and shimmer that moved his heart to bliss. "There goes dear Uncle Wolfe, sallying forth for a stroll. I think I'll offer to go with him."

"What a restless fellow you are, Tony. Why? He's probably only going down to the chemist."

"The chemist doesn't live in that direction," observed Anthony shrewdly. "I should say myself he wanted a little consolation."

Much later that night Derek came to a similar conclusion. Rounding a corner of the passage on his way to bed he almost cannoned against Wolfe, who was creeping along in stockinged feet.

"My dear boy," stammered Wolfe, "what on earth . . . You haven't been into Bertha, surely! I thought she was going to sleep."

"I expect she is. No, I haven't been near her. I'm not one of her favourites, you know."

"You shouldn't talk like that," said Wolfe uneasily. "She's a very queer woman. Why, I don't understand her after being married to her for nearly ten years. She hasn't been saying anything special to you, has she now?"

"She doesn't notice I'm about as a rule," exclaimed Derek gravely. "You look rather like the burglar of fiction yourself," he added with a grin. "Are you playing ghosts or something?"

"I thought the whole house was asleep. And I wanted to get myself something to drink." He coloured slightly. He could never accustom himself to the thought that he was legally master here.

Derek threw back his head and laughed softly. "Do you think I could have one, too?"

"I don't see why not. For goodness sake, boy, don't make all that noise. Would you have the whole house on us?"

"I dare say they'd all appreciate something to drink. Have you got the keys?"

"It's not all locked up," said Wolfe evasively. Derek looked at him with honest admiration. "Have you been able to hide some where she hasn't been able to find it? Good for you, Uncle Wolfe."

Together, Wolfe going silently in an agony of nervousness, Derek cool and self-possessed, they went downstairs. Wolfe produced some rum and two glasses.

"Late to be taking that," suggested Derek. "It must be midnight."

"It makes me sleep," Wolfe asserted, helping himself to a large tot. "Go on, lad, help yourself."

"I think, on second thoughts, I won't," decided Derek. "Salaams, Uncle Wolfe. Don't wake grandma on your way up."

As he bounded silently up the stairs he heard a door above him open and Anthony strolled out in a very startling dressing-gown designed in magenta and silver.

"What's in the wind? Is some one being foully done to death?"

"I don't think so. Only Uncle Wolfe feeling thirsty. He's swilling quarts of rum. What a palate!"

"My mother had a sister who drank tea at two every morning. She thought it was an adventure," confessed Anthony courageously. "Both habits are pretty nauseating, but I think I enrol myself under dear uncle's banner. Hallo! what's that? Didst thou not hear a noise?"

"I heard the owl scream and the cricket's cry," capped Derek neatly but inaccurately. "No, it's only Uncle Wolfe after all. And I believe you were right about the quarts of rum. I beg your pardon. I thought you were exaggerating."

"You'd better get out of sight, Tony. If he sees

you in that dressing-gown he'll think it's too good to be true."

"I suppose it wouldn't be the work of an honest man to try to touch him for a tenner just now? Even though I believe I possess his guilty secrets."

"What are they?"

"Wait till the morning. I shall have thought up some more picturesque details by then. They shall be very rich, I promise you, richer even than this gown, which incidentally was presented to me by a lady admirer in Streatham. The note was signed Lulu."

When Wolfe gained the landing a moment later walking with an extravagant caution, there was no one to be seen.

II

One other thing of moment happened that night. The final clause of the old gipsy's prophecy, that had made the stranger shudder, was fulfilled, and Bertha John died—of treachery—in a house where she had many kindred and no friend.

CHAPTER V

I

CAROL made the discovery just before seven o'clock on the morning of Wednesday, the 26th October. Coming into her grandmother's room to prepare her for the day, she was shocked and appalled by the sight of the great rigid body sprawled over the bed. It was obvious at once to her experience that her grandmother had died some hours ago. The huge red face was half-buried in the pillow, the golden wig she wore at night was thrust askew, her stout ungainly body lay at a peculiar angle, half-covered by the clothes, the eyes were wide open. They were strange eyes, black and long and narrow, set under black brows. Cruel eyes they had been when occasion warranted, cunning, pitiless, sardonic by turns; never merry or careless or roving to catch any expression or chance trail of beauty in the everyday world.

Carol stood rigid for a moment. At that instant her face wore an expression no one else ever saw. Hunted, apprehensive, terrified—and full of a furtive caution. Lifting her head she looked round the stuffy overfurnished room. Then, with a long breath, she went down the passage to Norman's door.

II

Norman, a methodical and early riser, had reached the shirt and trouser stage of his dressing, when he was disturbed by her knock.

"Oh, come in," he called, and Carol entered.

"I'm sorry, Norman, but something's happened. Will you come?"

Norman buttoned his waistcoat, pulling it down round his slender hips.

"Grandmother? Not a relapse!"

"I think she's dead."

"Good Lord!" He flashed a glance at Carol's stone-white face. "You weren't there or anything?"

"I've only just gone in. I thought at first she was still asleep."

Norman had caught up his coat and now they were walking side by side along the passage. "Heart, I suppose?" he hazarded. "I've never examined her professionally. Was her heart bad?"

"I didn't think it would give out suddenly like this."

.They reached their grandmother's room and Norman pushed open the door. The old woman, he saw at once, had been dead probably for a couple of hours. "Died in her sleep," he agreed. "We'd better phone Marshall. I can't butt in on this case. Get him, will you, Car?"

When Carol came back he said, smoothing his clean-shaven chin, "I suppose he'll give a certificate without any trouble? We don't want an inquest."

"I expect it will be all right. But why should you mind an inquest. There's no suspicion of foul play."

He looked at her sharply. "What makes you say that?"

"Well—you were so queer about an inquest, as if it would be disadvantageous."

"I don't say it would be disastrous, of course, but I think it would be very unfortunate, in the light of what happened last night."

"Unfortunate for whom?"

"Rose for one. Well, think for yourself. We were all sent for because grandmother was supposed to be dying, she made a marvellous recovery, and then, knowing the state of her health, Rose makes a priceless scene and upsets grandmother like Hades. You know she did. Did she say anything to you about it afterwards ? "

Carol looked wretched. " We—we had a bit of a row ourselves."

Norman suppressed his instinctive exclamation, " And you a nurse ! " and asked instead, " Why ? Anything important ? "

" I suppose I was a fool," Carol admitted. " But I had a vile headache—you know grandmother's practice of keeping all her windows hermetically sealed, as though fresh air were poisonous, so that, when they are opened, they creak and jam and take about three people to shut them ? And I'd been with her practically all day. So I was prepared to make heavy weather over what was probably mere exasperation on her part."

" What did she say ? "

" She was simply beastly about Derek, said that if I married him she'd cut me out of her will."

" She said that, Car ? "

" Well, practically. Anyhow, she talked of him being the type of young man that would like to live on a rich wife. I told her that people like us, who hadn't any special gifts, might be glad of the chance to be of use to exceptional people like Derek."

" A word in your ear," said Norman dryly. " If there should be an inquest, don't enlarge on the subject. People have such nasty minds."

" You mean, they might think I'd deliberately tried to upset her because if she didn't die in the night I'd be penniless. Oh! but that's too far-fetched, Norman."

"Just as you like," said Norman non-committally. "I've given you my advice. Go on."

"There really isn't any more. I think she was furious I was going to marry him. She'd never liked Derek. Aunt Dorothy had let it out. I said of course she must do as she pleased with her money, but nothing she did would prevent me and Derek marrying."

"Did she get much worked up over it?"

"I think so. Anyway, she told Dr. Marshall when he came. He seemed to think I'd make a fool of myself. That's his car now, isn't it?"

"Is it? By jove, the fellow's been quick. Perhaps he expected something of this kind."

The big fresh-coloured man came into the room. "What's up?" he asked. "A relapse." He frowned as he saw the huddled body in the bed. "When did this happen?"

"We found her like this—at least, I did. She seemed all right last night. I gave her a quarter of morphia as you said, and she seemed to settle down at once. I peeped in about half-past eleven, I didn't put on a light, but I could hear her breathing and she seemed all right. I usually come in about seven if she hasn't rung. When I saw her I realised something had happened, and I fetched my cousin."

Marshall, who had met Norman before, nodded, without relaxing his scowl.

"What am I supposed to put on the death certificate?" he demanded. "You know, she oughtn't to have gone like this. Did anything at all happen after I left last night?"

"Nothing."

"No one else came in to see her?"

"No—at least, so far as I know, they didn't. I went for a walk with my cousin."

"The black sheep?" The doctor's frown relaxed for an instant.

"Derek. I don't think any one would come in —or dare to—after grandmother was settled for the night."

"H'm. Well, I'd like to avoid an inquest if possible—you know how village people gossip, and there's probably been a deal too much talk already about family feeling in this house, all over the neighbourhood. But I have to admit I'm not satisfied. Hallo!" He bent over the bed. "Funny thing! Did she usually take two combs to bed with her?"

"Two? No, she had a white one . . ."

"I can see that. It's on the bedside-table. Whose is this?" From the creases of the coverlet he picked up a short black pocket-comb. Carol stared at it. "I don't recognise it. It might be practically any one's."

"It might. It's rather important, though, to find out whose. It looks to me as if some one did come in here last night, after you'd settled the old lady. You couldn't help noticing that if you'd seen it on the bed."

"It didn't fall out of your pocket, Norman, this morning when you bent over her?" suggested Carol.

" I don't carry such a thing, and if I did I don't think I'd choose mine at Skepworth's. That thing's got threepenny tray stamped all over it."

" We'll have to make inquiries about that," said the doctor, looking graver than ever. " You took her temperature last thing ? "

" Yes. It was quite normal. I've got the chart." She went away and came back with it and with the morphia phial, laying both on a small table near the window. The doctor picked up the chart and examined it professionally.

" There's really nothing new since I was in last night. She was subject, I know, to these sudden changes of temperature, and a woman of her unstable temperament is always liable to unexpected collapse, but that generally takes the form of a stroke or an apoplectic fit, and there are no traces of anything of that sort here. By the way, have you said anything to the rest of the household ? "

" Not yet."

" I suppose they should be told. And I think, too, we ought to trace the ownership of the comb. It looks uncommonly to me as though some one did come in here after Mrs. Wolfe had settled down for the night, and there may quite likely have been some kind of scene that would bring about this result. Anyhow, it's a possibility we can't let slide."

" I'll tell them what's happened," offered Norman. " Will you bring up the matter of the comb ? "

Marshall frowned. " Some one must. This isn't a police case, not yet anyhow. But whether I should do it—and in any case I ought to be over at

Woden Cross. There's been a serious accident there. They rang me up before I came over here."

"Anyway, I'll tell them," said Norman.

"Could you arrange for me to have some room where I could see people for a minute or two?" Marshall asked Carol.

"There's grandmother's sitting-room. I should think that would be all right. I'll see if Margaret's lighted a fire." She went away quickly, her mind full of doubt. Sometimes she had let herself dream of the carefree life that would be possible to her as a well-to-do woman, but now that the morning of her freedom had dawned she knew nothing but apprehension.

III

Norman was coming up from the dining-room where Derek had been sitting down to a hasty meal as Carol came back from her errand.

"I've arrested the lot," he called out.

Carol winced. "I don't suppose they need really stay long. I know Derek's frightfully busy. But it would be nice if Rose would stay. This is rather an alarming house at the moment."

"Don't answer this if you'd rather not," said Norman gently. "But what are you afraid of? Is it Derek?"

She tried to laugh off her fear. "I'm such a fool—superstitious and all that. I expect you're sick of women with nervous complexes, spending your life among them as you do. But—it's just coincidence,

I know, but I don't like it—Derek said last night, while we were waiting for the doctor to come down, and I'd told him about grandmother being in such a stew: 'Well, never mind. Don't let's worry to-night. Perhaps she'll die in her sleep.'"

"When was this?"

"Oh, about half-past nine. Dr. Marshall was pretty late coming over. I remember grandmother saying he was probably gallivanting with that girl he's going to marry, and she thought it absurd a man of his age behaving like a love-sick boy. But I think he's rather attractive, and you can't think of him as a man of fifty. Anyway, Hilary Musgrave's twenty-eight."

"My dear Carol, you really cannot expect me to be interested in the spectacle of Marshall as a ladies' man. Did Derek say anything else incriminating?"

"We'd just agreed that grandmother's cutting me out of her will shouldn't affect us . . ."

"I should have thought that was a matter beyond your jurisdiction. I don't see how it could help affecting you."

"In essentials, I mean."

"Derek knew about the money, then?"

"I'd just told him. I was turned out of the sick-room when the doctor came, so I sat in the hall. I thought if I went upstairs I should drop asleep, I was so tired. And the doctor might want to tell me something. I thought I'd wait till he'd gone, and then give grandmother her invalid food, that Margaret had put all ready outside her door, just before he arrived, and then I was going out for a little bit with Derek. We really hadn't seen one another since he came down here. Presently I heard steps coming downstairs; they paused by grandmother's door and then they came on. That was Derek. He said, 'I thought you were in there, when I heard voices. Who is it?' I said, 'Marshall,' and told him what had happened. He said, 'Oh, that must be what they're talking about so ardently. I heard something about not marrying on her forty thousand pounds.' And then he asked me if grandmother had really meant to leave me all that. I didn't know, of course. She's never mentioned an actual sum. It hardly seems as if there could be so much money in the world."

"And then did he make his indiscreet suggestion?"

"About grandmother dying in the night? Yes, I think he did. He didn't seem nearly so worried as I expected. Perhaps he thought she'd have changed her mind by this morning. It's all right, Norman. Don't look so serious. You know how Derek always talks."

"Oh, I do. But other people don't always, and misconceptions arise so easily. Good Lord, what I could do with a quarter of that money!" He brooded for an instant. "Anything else?"

"No. Norman, you don't really think we're going to have trouble over this?"

"Candidly, I don't. But Marshall did look a bit perturbed. And I shouldn't have said he was the sort of man to get the wind up easily."

"Can I have that room now?" Marshall asked, as the pair returned. "What about the husband? You've told him?"

Norman experienced his usual sensation of surprise at the thought of the handsome tongue-tied nonentity being this woman's mate. "Yes. He nearly came out of his skin at the news."

"H'm. Say anything about wanting to see her?"

"I don't think it occurred to him."

"Still it may." He walked over to the bed. "I think we ought to make things as pleasant for him as we can. At the moment . . ."

They were all silent for an instant, looking at the sprawled, ungainly figure, with its red face slipped sideways on the pillow. The eyes were wide and staring. Something about them made Norman say suddenly, "She must have been worse than I thought. She's had a lot of morphia."

"What's that?" Marshall bent over the body. There was a slow pause. Then he straightened himself and spoke to Carol.

"How much did you give her last night?" he asked.

"A quarter, as you said." Carol sounded surprised.

"H'm, the pupils are so contracted, I thought——" He straightened himself, looking rather embarrassed. "Where is the phial?"

"I brought it in and put it on that table."

Marshall picked it up and held it up to the light. "I gave you five grains, didn't I? That seems about right." But he turned and looked at the body in a perplexed manner as if something troubled him. Then in an instant his face changed. He uncorked the little phial, stood for a moment a picture of massive incredulity, then turned back to Carol.

His expression was curious ; it wasn't condemnatory in the least ; it was almost pitiful, and he touched her arm with a gesture that held only kindness as he said, " My dear, you'll have to explain this."

" Explain ? " All the fears that had overtaken her in the passage rushed back to assault her anew.

" Why this phial's full of water."

Carol looked at them both dizzily. Each wore the same expression, forbearing and gentle ; but behind that was something implacable. She heard herself cry, " Don't look at me like that. I don't know what you mean."

Norman grasped her arm firmly. " Pull yourself together, Car. No good going to pieces now. And don't talk. You've had a shock. Marshall thinks, and I agree with him, that the police will have to be called in. I'm going to phone for them now."

" But I've nothing to hide," Carol protested in bewildered tones.

" Of course not. But—I'm speaking professionally, you understand—when one's knocked suddenly off one's balance, as you've been, one's apt to say things that are liable to misconstruction, not to any of us, but to outsiders, the people who mould public opinion."

" There are none of them here."

" If this becomes a public inquiry, and it looks as if it will, we shall all be put through the mangle. They'll want to know word for word what every one said at the moment of the discovery, and so forth. See ? "

" Your cousin's right," Marshall added soberly.

"You've said you're all at sea. That's enough for the present. And now I'm afraid I must get along to Woden Cross. I've probably wrecked my reputation as it is. If I'm wanted in a hurry during the next half-hour or so, you'll get me at the Cottage Hospital. They take all these road accidents there. But I don't suppose you will."

CHAPTER VI

THE inquest was held on Friday (the death had been discovered on Wednesday morning); people in the neighbourhood whispered hopefully that it usually meant something queer when the inquest was so long postponed. The members of the family had preserved a stolid silent solidity as they moved among their acquaintances. None of them had been back to London, and in the minds of more than one was a secret speculation as to how many of them would be free to return to London when the inquest was over.

During its progress they were accommodated in a room outside the court, while the preliminaries were examined. Norman, who had kept his head throughout, had telephoned to a man they all knew, a solicitor called Rupert Neville, to come down and watch the case for the family. No one had even murmured his or her fears to any other member of the party, but they went about looking rather haggard, and didn't meet one another's eyes with their normal candour, presumably because they were afraid of betraying their suspicions.

"Why aren't we allowed in the court to hear what the doctor and the police are saying?" Carol wanted to know.

"They want to hear our separate versions," Derek said grimly. "It's the story of Susannah and the Elders over again."

"But we might agree all to tell the same story. Wouldn't that come to the same thing?"

"We can't be absolutely certain what questions they're going to ask. They may spring an odd one to any one of us that has never occurred to our minds. They're playing for safety, of course."

Carol lay back. She looked white and exhausted. "I suppose they're right."

Rose, as carefully made-up as usual, and speaking with her customary energy and sparkle, said, "Car, did they ask you about that comb?"

"Yes. It wasn't mine, though."

"It wasn't mine, either, but I had to empty my bag and show them that I'd got a comb with me—do they think that hair does itself?—and then they said had I got another, and did I ever use a black comb . . . ?"

"Yes, they asked me all that, too."

"What men escape," said Rose.

"We didn't," returned Derek gloomily. "At least, I didn't. I suppose they think all men who write novels run combs through their hair while waiting for the soup in their bohemian restaurants. If they only knew that the one place where you won't find writers are these bohemian dens, which incidentally are the resort of the suburbs. Naturally. If I have another existence, I'm going on the Stock Exchange. It's less open to misconstruction."

Marshall gave his evidence in much detail. He said that the examination of the body had revealed the fact that the deceased had undoubtedly died from an overdose of morphia.

The coroner interrupted to say, in his precise, clipped voice, "I think, before we get any further, Dr. Marshall, there is one point that should be definitely settled. Is there any possibility that Mrs. Wolfe took her own life?"

Marshall frowned. "It seems to me highly improbable, if, indeed, it isn't out of the question. I don't know where she could obtain the morphia."

"She couldn't have been a secret addict?"

"I'm afraid that's hardly likely," said Marshall dryly. "I had been her medical attendant for some years, and I think it is impossible that she should have contracted this habit without my becoming aware of it."

"I asked the question so as to give the jury an opportunity of forming their opinion as easily as possible. Since you definitely rule out the possibility, I suppose we must take it that the morphia was administered by some other person, either wilfully or by accident."

"It seems like it," the doctor agreed.

"Then, having disposed of that point, perhaps you will tell the jury in your own words what happened, so far as you know. When did you last see Mrs. Wolfe alive?"

"At about nine o'clock on the night before her death. I had promised Miss Carol that I would look in, though I hardly thought it necessary, Mrs. Wolfe being so much better. I shouldn't have been surprised to hear that she had settled down for the night before my arrival."

"But this wasn't the case?"

"On the contrary, I found her very excited and talkative."

"And that surprised you?"

"Not altogether. When a woman is as much accustomed to having her own way on every occasion as Mrs. Wolfe, the smallest upset to her plans, or any show of opposition, will bring about something in the nature of a scene."

"And you gathered there had been some sort of opposition that evening?"

Dr. Marshall turned squarely to the jury. "I should like the jury to understand quite clearly that they are not in this case dealing with a perfectly normal woman. I'm aware that that is a dangerous thing to say, and perhaps I ought to qualify it. I don't for one instant mean to suggest that she was certifiable or had any mental disease, but you couldn't appeal to her normality as you can to the normality of the majority of people. She had what nowadays we call a complex—and that complex was power. She wanted to govern and possess other people; sometimes that can be done by personal charm or by exerting some impulse of affection. But in her case neither of those ways was possible. But she had one weapon that she considered, and with some justice, extremely powerful. She was wealthy, and all her relatives, even if they didn't actively need money, wanted it. She expected to be able to wield authority for that reason. She was as fierce as the mediæval Church confronted with the unblushing atheist when she encountered people who wouldn't pay due respect to her idols. I put that very strongly, but, if I don't, it will be difficult for any one to understand how much value to place on her remarks and criticisms. I would like to urge the jury to take her sweeping comments on the probable action and reactions of her own circle with a large pinch of salt. I do here speak from personal conviction."

There was a moment's silence. Every one knew of the tragedy to which he made covert reference. Rather more than a year ago, Dr. Marshall's sister, an amiable spinster living in the district, had come under Mrs. Wolfe's magnetic spell. It hadn't been possible in this instance to hold out money as a bait, because Miss Marshall, though less well-off than Mrs. Wolfe, had a handsome fortune of her own. But she was not very strong-willed, and she easily became dominated by her ruthless neighbour. The district spoke of it, Dr. Marshall was uneasy, the more so when his sister, who had all her life been a devout woman, suddenly thrust her religion aside and announced that she was free at last of such superstitions. The outcome had been pure tragedy. For some months Miss Marshall had gone abroad, blatant in her atheism; then one night she flung herself out of a window, leaving a dishevelled, barely decipherable note to the effect that, as there was no longer a God to believe in, she didn't want to live.

"During the course of this inquiry," Marshall

continued, after a moment's pause, "it's probable you will hear a lot of rather wild talk about ingratitude and alteration of wills and so forth. I don't want you to pay too much attention to all that. Mrs. Wolfe didn't mean a great deal of it, any more than she meant a great deal of what she said in ordinary everyday conversation. That's just a warning against taking every chance word too seriously. The actual hunger for power over other people had become an obsession with her by this time. She had to go on governing people, even after she was dead. That's why she kept altering her will, keeping her beneficiaries in suspense."

"Thank you, Dr. Marshall." That was the coroner, curt and repressive. "I think the jury has quite grasped your point. Now perhaps you will tell them precisely what it was that Mrs. Wolfe wished to say to you in secret on that last night."

"She told me that she had been upset, that all her relatives were ungrateful, that they only cared for her money, and that if she were a poor woman there wasn't one of them who wouldn't put the telegrams in the basket and let her die alone."

"Did she mention any specific names?"

"She said that she'd been deceived even in her favourite grandchild, but that she wasn't dead yet nor a fool, and there was still time to escape from her Fool's Paradise."

"Did she say exactly what she meant by that?"

"I gather she intended to make yet another alteration in her will. It had become quite a habit of hers."

" Did she say anything definite about the proposed changes ? "

" She said she was going to cut all of her relations out of her will and leave every stiver to a home for lost dogs. She'd heard that dogs were affectionate by nature, and not calculating, like human beings. That's typical of her illogical attitude when she was upset. I stayed with her about twenty minutes, but I didn't attempt to argue with her. She wasn't in a fit state to be thwarted. I didn't want to be up with her half the night myself or have her keeping her household on the run till dawn. I thought probably if she were allowed to fulminate she'd soon cool down. I met Miss Carol in the hall and told her what I thought. I said she'd better give her a morphia injection, a quarter of a grain ; I knew she had enough, as I had given her five grains two days earlier. Mrs. Wolfe had it when she had these attacks, and it seemed to me particularly important that she should sleep well that night."

" You didn't think it necessary for her to have any one in her room ? "

" I thought it definitely better for her to be alone. She was making the most unreasonable accusations against Miss Carol, who would be the obvious person to sleep with her, and I didn't want her to go on all night. If I had thought it necessary for her to have a companion, I'd have sent in a nurse ; but there was no ground for any such action so far as I could see. To my mind she merely needed sleep."

" Quite. And when you spoke to Miss Carol about her grandmother's condition, did she seem at all upset or strange in her manner ? "

" She was anxious, in a professional way. No nurse likes her patient to get into such a state. In a sense, it's a criticism of her ability to manage her charge. One of the first essential qualities for a nurse is the tact required to keep a tiresome patient calm, but in fairness to Miss Carol, I ought to add that there are cases, and I think Mrs. Wolfe was one, where it's sometimes impossible to accomplish this."

" Did she mention her discussion with her grandmother of her own accord ? "

" Yes, though she didn't go into details. Mrs. Wolfe did that."

" And what did she say ? "

" That she disapproved of Miss Carol's proposed marriage, and was inclined to disinherit her if she persisted in the idea. But that may all have been hot air. It's wonderful how the new day restores people to sanity. And in any case it was never safe to attach too much importance to anything Mrs. Wolfe might say when she was upset."

He then, at the instigation of the coroner, spoke of his summons, his examination of the body, and his surprise at discovering the condition of the pupils that gave him his first clue as to the actual cause of death. He had naturally been anxious to avoid an inquest, as this entailed a good deal of very undesirable publicity, and for certain members of the household the ordeal would have been a very disagreeable one.

" Will you tell the jury what you wish them to understand by that, Dr. Marshall ? " rasped the fierce little coroner.

" It's simple enough, sir. The mere mention of

an inquest suggests foul play to numbers of people, and with so many men and women in the house, who either hoped or expected to benefit by her death, particularly having regard to the local gossip regarding her, it was bound to cause a lot of unpleasantness. If the jury consider the position for a moment, they'll grasp my point, I know. Whenever a rich person dies at all unexpectedly, when he's surrounded by poor relatives, and it's known that none of them were what we might call devoted to him, tongues begin to wag. Particularly in villages where there's less to distract people's minds than in the case of towns. Of course, there are times when an inquest is inevitable, but naturally whenever it's possible I dispense with it for the sake of the family."

"Thank you, Dr. Marshall. I think we understand your point now. Did the family make any suggestions?"

"Miss Carol said doubtfully, Was it a stroke? And Dr. Bell suggested heart failure. But as a matter of fact, Mrs. Wolfe had a very strong heart; she'd have been dead years ago but for that. I admit I was perplexed. Some rumour of the truth was going round the house—presumably the servants knew I had come and realised something serious was up. Various members of the family began to come downstairs and Dr. Bell said he'd tell them what had happened. I understand that most, if not all, of them were arranging to return to town that morning, and were probably catching the first train. I looked at my watch, and saw that they wouldn't have long if they really meant to go up by that, and I wanted to see them before they went."

"Why was that? Did you expect foul play?"

"No. Miss Carol had already asked me that, and I said I saw no reason for such a suggestion. All the same, as the dead woman's doctor, I thought I should make a little inquiry. A doctor, you'll realise, has to consider his own reputation as well as every one else's, and if there's a shadow of a doubt in any one's mind as to how even the most insignificant patient meets his death, he's got to leave no stone unturned to establish the truth. And here I had a woman, dying very unexpectedly, a woman of great importance locally, whose death would be much discussed. I didn't, I admit, suspect any hole-and-corner work—I thought it was a case of sudden collapse, which does happen sometimes when you least expect it—but for formality's sake I thought I should see the various relatives before they left the house."

He then went on to explain how he had attempted to straighten the body to afford as little shock as possible to the dead woman's husband, and while he was doing so Dr. Bell had been struck by the appearance of the dead woman. He (witness) had therefore examined the morphia phial, wondering if Miss Carol could have administered a larger injection than she intended. It was then he had discovered that the phial had been tampered with and water substituted for the drug.

"What did Miss Carol say when you pointed this out?"

"She looked astounded, and she shivered a little;

but then the window was open and the morning was very cold. She said she knew nothing of the affair and was as perplexed as myself. Of course, in the light of this information I realised that an inquest would be inevitable. And when it was held it was obvious that Mrs. Wolfe had had three or four grains of morphia injected shortly before her death."

CHAPTER VII

CAROL had been called and was now giving evidence. She agreed that she was a granddaughter of the deceased, and had been employed by her on various occasions in her professional capacity. The last occasion had been on the Thursday evening preceding Mrs. Wolfe's death.

"You were, therefore, accustomed to her symptoms?" the coroner suggested.

"Yes."

"And it was doubtless for this reason that she preferred you to a stranger?"

"She hated strangers. She didn't see the use of having professionals in the family if you couldn't call on them in emergencies."

The people in the court, that was crowded, turned to look at one another with some disapproval. Two ladies in fur tippets confided audibly to one another that this wasn't the way to talk of the dead. They began to think, before another word was spoken, that this young woman probably wasn't all she looked.

"I see. Now I understand that on this occasion your grandmother had been seriously ill?"

"Yes. She had these bouts."

"You thought it might be fatal?"

"There was always the possibility that she might collapse. But I had nursed her through similar attacks before."

"So you weren't really anxious?"

"There's always a certain amount of anxiety in circumstances like that."

"But not sufficient to justify your sleeping with her, for instance?"

"The doctor thought it unnecessary."

"In the circumstances it must have come as a great shock to you when you found next day that she was dead."

"It was a great shock. She had seemed so much better the night before."

"You don't think that perhaps she had been allowed to overdo it? These sudden rallies are very deceptive. And perhaps she talked too much, got excited?"

"She did get rather excited."

"Ah! Now what was it precisely that excited her?"

Carol became more vague. "She really liked to think that she had the power to spring these surprises on us."

"Spring these surprises, Miss John? That's rather a peculiar expression, surely. I'm afraid I must ask you to explain."

"All my cousins had to stop work at short notice and come down to Aston Merry," explained Carol.

"It had happened before when there had seemed a possibility of our grandmother's death. And she had always got better. I mean, I think she liked to feel that though she was older and to some extent power was passing out of her hands, she could still exercise power over us." She finished lamely. The feeling of the court would have been obvious to a blind man.

"I see," said the coroner in a slow voice. Close beside him was a man from the local police force, who was watching her narrowly. Carol felt suddenly very hot, clammy with heat, as one does before sea-sickness. "Well, we'll leave that point. What I want to establish is whether there was any particular subject that excited Mrs. Wolfe the evening before her death. Or any particular person."

"N-no," said Carol, so hesitantly that the coroner thought the time had come to warn her that she was in a very serious position, giving evidence in a mysterious death inquest, and that she should weigh her words with care. "Perhaps it would be best if you were to repeat such of the conversation as you can remember. Mrs. Wolfe had, perhaps, an argument with some member of the family."

There wasn't, Carol thought, any need to implicate Rose. It wasn't Rose who had had the final word. So she acknowledged slowly, "We had a—a sort of discussion while I was getting her to bed. She inaugurated it. . . ."

"What was this discussion about?"

"Well—money, I suppose, really."

"Money, you suppose. Mrs. Wolfe's money?"

"Y-yes."

"Oh, and how did you come to be discussing that?"

"She spoke of it."

"In what connection?"

Carol considered. The events of that night and the following morning were becoming blurred in her memory now, and for the first time she began to be afraid of giving false evidence. A slip was so easy to make, and they'd pounce on you and never let you forget. The coroner repeated his question rather testily. "I'm sorry. I was trying to remember exactly how the point cropped up. I think we were talking about security, whether it was good for people to know they were safe, financially, I mean, and I thought it was."

"And your grandmother disagreed?"

"Yes. She said the strain and anxiety of bread-winning were stimulating. She's never been poor herself, you see."

"Well, that's a matter of opinion. How did you get on to the question of her money?"

"She said I should be a fool if I let my husband rest on what I had."

"Meaning the legacy she intended to leave you?"

"I suppose so. She knew I had nothing of my own but what I earned."

"And what did you say to her last remark?"

"That I didn't think the man I was going to marry would want to be supported by his wife."

"And then?"

"She asked me who he was."

"And you told her?"

"My cousin, Mr. Blake. I think it was rather a shock to her."

"Should you say a pleasant shock?"

"No. She despises writers and people like that."

"And she was dismayed at the prospect of her money passing into the hands of a writer's wife?"

"Yes. She said she might as well leave it to foreign missions or to Margaret Grant—that's the servant she has had for a dozen years or more."

"She actually threatened to alter her will?"

"Yes. But she'd done that before."

"But she did do it on this occasion? Did she say in what direction she would alter it?"

Carol remained silent.

"Miss John, you must realise that you are here to give evidence and to answer such questions as are put to you. Did Mrs. Wolfe say anything definite as to what alterations she might make?"

"She said she wouldn't let her money be squandered like that."

"Meaning that she was going to cut you out of her will altogether?"

"It might have meant that. You couldn't tell with grandmother. She'd often say things at night that she'd forgotten by the morning."

"Did she speak of sending for her solicitor?"

"He was coming anyhow the next day."

"She didn't mention him then at this juncture?"

"I—believe she did."

"You believe? Miss John, is it possible that you do not realise how important it is that we should have the facts clearly crystallised? We wish to know precisely what your grandmother said."

"It isn't so easy to remember every word after several days of being harried and examined and questioned," cried poor Carol passionately. "I think she did say it was as well Mr. Nicholls was coming over."

"She said that, and you still didn't think she was serious?"

"I didn't know. I've said she might be."

"Did you speak of this to any one?"

"Only to Mr. Blake."

"And he said . . .?"

"He was sure she'd have changed her mind in the morning."

"I wonder why he thought that. Had Mrs. Wolfe threatened to disinherit you on any other occasion?"

"No, I don't think so."

"Not once."

"Not that I remember."

"And, of course, you would remember a threat of that nature?"

"Of course."

"So that the position on the 25th October was more grave than it had ever been before?"

"Yes. Yes, it may have been."

"Thank you. Now then, you say you gave Mrs. Wolfe a morphia injection last thing at night?"

"Yes. Dr. Marshall had ordered it. A quarter of a grain."

"Where did you keep this morphia?"

"In my room."

"Where any one could tamper with it?"

"No. I kept it locked up. And I kept the key."

"So that no one but yourself had access to it?"

"No."

"On the 25th October when you came to give the injection, you would have noticed if any attempt had been made to tamper with the drawer or cabinet where it was kept?"

"I suppose so. Though I couldn't be certain. I was feeling rather upset. . . ."

"On account of your grandmother's behaviour?"

"Partly that. Partly I was horribly tired. Anyway, I just unlocked the drawer and measured out the amount, and then I carried the syringe along to my grandmother's room."

"Did you see any one on the way?"

"Only Margaret Grant going up to bed."

"What time was this?"

"I should think about nine forty-five. The doctor had been here quite a long time."

"I see. Then, after you returned to your grandmother's room, did you have any more conversation with her?"

"We didn't go back to the topic of her will. She asked for one or two things, and told me some orders she wanted given in the morning—just household things. Then I gave her the invalid food and directly after that the injection, and then she settled down to sleep. When I looked in about half-past eleven she hadn't moved."

"And when you left her?"

"I went back to my room, and then I went for a walk."

"Alone?"

"No, with Mr. Blake. We'd arranged to get a

half-hour together if we could, as he had to go back to town early next morning."

"I see. Now, did you tell Mr. Blake what your grandmother had said about the legacy?"

"I think I said—'Oh, I believe I've lost you that money.'"

"Wasn't that rather an odd way of putting it, seeing the money was to be yours?"

"What I meant was that if grandmother did carry out her threat, we couldn't be married yet."

Rupert Neville stifled a groan at that reply. Like all solicitors, his worst clients were those who would be transparently honest.

"I see. And of course you were anxious to marry this young man as soon as possible."

"Of course."

"But without that money, had you any idea how long you might have to wait?"

"Until Mr. Blake was earning enough by his books to support a wife."

"Did he say anything when you told him the news?"

"He said, 'Well, it doesn't matter either way. I'm doing a new book now that I'm sure will be successful, and we can be married in about a year.'"

"He has no definite proof of this book's success?"

"How can he when it isn't even out yet? It isn't finished."

"So he was simply being optimistic. He has, perhaps, felt like that about other books of his?"

"I've never heard him say so."

She thought he would never let her go, and when at last he seemed satisfied there was Rupert Neville on his feet, long and cool and smiling, saying, "Now," Miss John, isn't it a fact that the doctor warned you your grandmother might last a great many years yet ? "

" He said she might go on another ten or fifteen ? "

" And during that time she might change her mind very often ? "

" She probably would."

" And you and Mr. Blake were not proposing to postpone your marriage so long ? "

" Of course not."

" And are you much given to brooding over the distant future ? "

Carol shook her head. " No. I'm fairly careful, I suppose."

He interrupted her smoothly. " Oh, quite. And I dare say you've saved quite a nice little nest-egg during these last ten years."

" Yes. I didn't mean to count on my grandmother, and I wanted to have something for emergencies."

" So that the problem of what Mrs. John might or might not leave you, say fifteen years hence, wouldn't trouble you to any very great extent at the present time ? I mean, for instance, it wouldn't affect your marriage either way ? "

The coroner disapproved of the leading nature of that question, and Neville amended it. But Carol had seen the drift of his examination and gave him the answer he wanted.

" There's one more thing, Miss John. When you went to your grandmother's room to give her the injection, did you lock up the phial of morphia before you went ? "

"No, I didn't. I didn't expect to be away more than a minute, and no one would go into my room. My grandmother hated to be kept waiting."

"Did you lock your door?"

"No. I just shut it."

"So that anybody could have gone in?"

"Yes, I suppose so. But why should they want to? They wouldn't know about the morphia."

"They might see you going to your grandmother's room, holding the syringe."

"Yes, they might do that, of course."

"And we know there were people about. You admit yourself you saw one of the servants going upstairs. And presumably the servants went to bed before the rest of the household. Probably the house was full of people at that time."

"I don't think any one was out."

"Precisely. So there was an opportunity for a determined person to abstract the morphia and fill up the phial with water. How long were you away?"

"About a quarter of an hour, as it happened."

"I see. And when you came back?"

"Mr. Blake and I went for a walk. I'd locked up the morphia by then, though."

"Oh, quite." He smiled at her and sat down. Perhaps after all that damning candour of hers might be brought to tell in her favour. You never could be sure.

Carol stumbled out of the court; it had been a hideous ordeal. She wondered how she had ever thought of herself as brave.

Carol went away and Wolfe took her place. He

was obviously distressed, so much so that the fur tippets whispered sagaciously that he looked the picture of guilt. But Neville, who had grown up in the country, knew the alarm and dread countrymen exhibit in the face of anything they cannot understand, and he thought you could explain Wolfe's expression in that way as well as any other.

Wolfe agreed that the dead woman was his wife, to whom he had been married for ten years. He said he had last seen her alive about seven o'clock on Tuesday night, when he had gone into her room to say good-night. There had been no conversation at that time.

"But you had had some conversation with your wife earlier in the day?"

"I had tea with her."

"Was any one else there?"

"No, not then."

"And did she speak of her will to you?"

"She'd never talk to me about her will."

"Did she tell you she'd sent for the lawyer?"

"No, not even that. I heard it by chance from one of her grandchildren."

"I see. Now, Mr. Wolfe, on that occasion you asked your wife to lend you money?"

"Twenty pounds. I had a gambling debt . . ."

"Did she agree to do so?"

"No, she hated gambling."

"She was annoyed?"

"She was furious. And, of course, I couldn't press the point with her being as ill as she was."

"But the debt was pressing?"

"Yes."

"Is it settled?"

"It is. I was able to get the money elsewhere?"

"From whom?"

Wolfe seemed more ill at ease than ever. At last he gulped out, "Well, from Dr. Bell, if you must know. Though I can't see what this has to do with Bertha's death."

"Was that at the same time as you asked him for the prescription for insomnia?"

"Yes. I was telling him I couldn't sleep."

"And I think you asked Mr. Whirter what was in the sleeping draught?"

"That's right."

"Why was that?"

"I like to know what I'm taking."

"And you asked him how many tablets a man would need to drop into a really heavy sleep?"

"Yes. I didn't want to go on lying awake all the rest of my life."

"Mr. Whirter warned you that it's only too easy to be the slave of these drugs."

"It's no worse than being the slave of insomnia. That's enough to drive a man mad."

"And then you asked him how many it would take to drug a man?"

"Yes. I just wanted to know. I didn't want to take too many."

"And you asked if it would be possible to kill a man with these tablets?"

"He said it wouldn't. They weren't strong enough."

"And then you began to talk to him about poisons generally?"

"Yes. I said I'd heard of a girl with a baby she didn't want taking a whole bottle of aspirin, and I said if it was as dangerous as that, she oughtn't to be able to get hold of it."

"No. You don't take aspirin yourself, Mr. Wolfe?"

"I don't. I've always regarded it as a sort of lady's fad, like smelling salts."

Some one laughed. The coroner said angrily that if he had any more disturbance he would clear the court. "There appear to be some persons present," he observed, "who have no conception of the gravity of the occasion. We are here to discover the truth regarding the death of a woman, well known, by reputation at all events, to us all, who has been furtively done to death, presumably by a member of her own household." He flushed a little when he had said that, as though realising that he had gone too far, then continued quickly, to Wolfe, "Now, Mr. Wolfe, you admit that you questioned Mr. Whirter rather closely about the nature and power of various poisons?"

"There's been a lot of cases in the paper lately, and I didn't want to take a fatal dose; and at the same time I didn't want to take just what would be enough for a baby or a schoolboy and not go to sleep any more than when I didn't have anything."

"I see. And Mr. Whirter explained to you that two tablets should certainly be sufficient?"

"He said so."

"But you resolved to take more?"

"He told me I couldn't poison myself if I did."

"And how many did you resolve to take?"

"Three, to be on the safe side." Wolfe, whose high colour seemed to glow as though with actual heat, spoke quickly and with defiance.

"So you took three? And what did you do with the bottle? Leave it lying about where anybody else could get hold of it?"

"No. I kept it on me."

"Why was that?"

"I wasn't going to have all the household saying I took drugs."

"Still, a sleeping-draught," the coroner began, but Wolfe interrupted him fiercely, "Do you think I don't know how people talk? I've lived in this village all my life. That's why I didn't want to get anything that 'ud actually be poisonous."

"I don't quite follow," said the coroner courteously.

Wolfe's self-control began to give way. "Think I can't see what you're driving at? What every one in this court's driving at? That it was me that tried to kill Bertha—or did kill her, for that matter? Well, it wasn't, and I wasn't going to give any one a chance of saying it was. So I got something that couldn't kill any one."

"You mean, that before there was any suggestion of Mrs. Wolfe being killed, you were on your guard against the possibility of such a suggestion?"

"If you'd lived my life, say the last five years, you'd be on your guard, too. Why, my wife was always taunting me with how I'd like to see her dead."

Neville frowned and drew a line of cats on the

sheet of paper in front of him. He wasn't here to defend Wolfe, but he thought some one might have warned the fellow not to give this gratuitous information to the court.

The coroner said smoothly, "So all your questions to Mr. Whirter arose from a developed caution?"

Wolfe repeated doggedly, "I wasn't going to give any of 'em a chance of saying I was bringin' poisons into the house."

"Well, we might leave that for the moment. Now, coming to the evening. What time did you retire?"

"Pretty early. That is, I went upstairs pretty early. I didn't take the tablets then."

"When did you take the tablets?"

"Oh, about midnight."

"And you took three?"

"That's right."

"Then can you explain why it is that there are six missing from the bottle?"

Wolfe stared; his face went a curious plum-purple. "Six—I—you don't know . . ."

"This is a quite common form of sleeping-draught. You don't actually need a prescription. The tablets are put up in quantities of twenty-five or fifty. You bought a bottle of twenty-five. You only used them one night——"

"I took three more the next night," broke in Wolfe, sweating.

"The police obtained possession of the little bottle on the Wednesday, that is the morning on which your wife was found dead. There were then nineteen tablets in the bottle."

There was a deathly silence in the court. " You've nothing to say ? " asked the coroner, inexorably.

" I can't explain, unless somebody got at the bottle."

" But no one would want to take sleeping-draughts in the morning."

" Well, I dunno. I just took the three."

" And can you explain how it is that the glass in your room had not been used ? The tablets have to be taken in water."

" Well, I didn't take mine in water. I was thirsty and I went down to get a drink."

" At midnight ? "

" About then. You could ask one of my wife's grandsons, Mr. Blake. He came with me, but he changed his mind at the last minute."

" And so you took them with—a whisky-and-soda, perhaps ? "

" No, with rum."

" Rum ? Isn't that rather a strange drink to take at that hour ? "

" I've always had a partiality for rum," said Wolfe doggedly. And then, flinging back his head, he shouted, " She kept everything else locked up. That's the kind of woman she was."

" Oh, I see. Then you took your three tablets with the rum. And then you went up to bed ?"

" Yes."

" And went to bed ? "

" Yes." A coarse sense of humour made him add, " No witness of that, I'm afraid."

The coroner leaned forward. " Then in that case, Mr. Wolfe, can you explain how it was that after taking a sleeping-draught fifty per cent. stronger than that normally taken, you were awake and alert by seven o'clock the next morning. There is evidence that you were on the scene of the death among the first. A doctor will agree that having taken so many you would at all events have been drowsy."

"It's what I've always said. These things don't work."

"I see. You swallowed them whole, or did you dilute them into the rum?"

"Oh, swallowed 'em whole."

"That is rather strange. You are interested in horse-racing, Mr. Wolfe?"

"Well, suppose I am?"

"You get the racing edition of the newspapers sometimes?"

"Not often. But my wife would never have the wireless."

"So you couldn't get the news that way. But on the day before she died, you bought a copy of the *Evening Record*?"

"I don't remember. I may have done."

"A copy was found in your bedroom. It would hardly have been put there by any one else."

"I suppose not. Well, then I bought it. I'm not one of your account keepers, knowing where every halfpenny's gone to."

The coroner held up a crumpled paper. "This is the paper in question."

"I daresay. One evening paper looks much the same as another, doesn't it?"

"This copy happens to have a piece torn off the

front page. You see." He exhibited the mutilated page for the benefit of the jury. "That missing scrap was found, Mr. Wolfe, in the waste paper basket in your room. In it were a few grains of a white powder. The paper itself had been doubled in two and there was a curious mark on one side." Again he produced a piece of paper and passed it to the foreman of the jury, who sent it on its gradual round. "The suggestion from that is that the tablets were ground to powder inside the fold of that piece of newspaper, probably with the heel of a boot or shoe. Further grains of the powder have been discovered in the folds of a clean handkerchief that had been hastily thrust into a drawer in your room."

"I don't know anything about all this," exploded Wolfe violently.

"And there's one other place where grains of this same powder have been discovered. And that is on the green wooden tray on which Mrs. Wolfe's invalid food was standing for about twenty minutes outside her door on the night of the 25th. The servant, Margaret Grant, told the authorities that she carried the tray up at nine-fifteen. Miss John said she took it in at about nine forty-five. The food had been mixed and placed in a covered metal vessel to keep it hot. Miss John usually stirred up the mixture and, of course, would not notice anything peculiar about it. Now, Mr. Wolfe, can you explain any of that?"

"It doesn't seem to me very difficult. Some one got at my bottle and took three tablets out, when I wasn't in the room. I didn't count how many tablets there were in the bottle. I didn't even know they'd been numbered."

"But of course you noticed that the paper seal had been broken when you came to open the bottle?"

Wolfe looked outnumbered. "I—I don't remember. I don't suppose I'd think of such a thing."

"And then I thought you said you kept the bottle in your pocket all the time?"

"During the evening. But I didn't take it downstairs with me when I went to get my drink. It was in my room then."

"But the powder had appeared on Mrs. Wolfe's tray three hours earlier."

"Well, some one else must have had some tablets. That's all I can say."

"I'm afraid you're not very convincing, Mr. Wolfe. However, we can leave that point to the jury. Now there is something else I must ask you to explain. On Mrs. Wolfe's bed was found a black pocket-comb that several witnesses have identified as being yours. Can you explain how it came to be where it was discovered?"

"I went in to say good-night to my wife, of course. And bending over her, I suppose it slipped out of my pocket."

"Were you the last person to see her?"

"Miss John was coming back to give her the injection, she said."

"She was waiting for her?"

"Yes."

"Sitting up and apparently quite cheerful?"

" Oh yes. I remember thinking how marvellous she was, seeing only forty-eight hours before every one had thought she was going to die."

" Then if she was sitting up, it seems strange that you should have to bend down so far that the comb would slip out of your waistcoat pocket. If you were a very tall man one might be ready to give it the benefit of the doubt, but—what height would you put yourself, Mr. Wolfe ? "

" I'm five foot nine."

" So that if you stooped to kiss your wife good-night—the bed, I understand, is not peculiarly low or anything of that nature—it would be surprising for the comb to slide out."

" Well, that's what must ha' happened. And I didn't notice it."

" Nor did Mrs. Wolfe."

" Well, she'd ha' told me if she had."

" Nor Miss John, apparently, though she says she was meticulous about straightening the bed before she left the room."

" A little thing like a comb could easy enough slip into a crease and not be noticed."

" And you hadn't realised that it was missing ? "

" No. Not till the police came asking if I'd ever seen it before."

" And you recognised it immediately ? "

" Yes. I felt in my pocket right away, and it wasn't there."

" And you still deny placing any of the sleeping-draught in your wife's invalid food ? "

" Certainly I do."

"Ah!" Wolfe was not the only person in court to feel the peculiarity of that ejaculation. The coroner continued smoothly, "I'm afraid I must detain you a little longer, Mr. Wolfe. You say you had been drinking rum?"

"A man can drink his own rum in his own house, surely?'"

"Why, of course, but two witnesses say there was a distinct smell of rum in Mrs. Wolfe's room the following morning."

"I don't know anything about that," shouted Wolfe sullenly. "It's not my fault that she keeps her windows tight shut. And I don't understand about the sleeping-draught or what you're trying to get at about the invalid food. I knew those tablets wouldn't poison any one, and anyway, my wife died of morphine poisoning. I hadn't got any morphine; I shouldn't know where to get it; and no one 'ud give it me."

And to no amount of questioning would he vouchsafe any other reply.

But still the coroner detained him.

"Of course, Mr. Wolfe, you realised that under your wife's will you'd benefit?"

"She always told me so, but I never knew anything for sure. She took care of that."

"Do you mean us to understand by that remark that your marriage was not a happy one?"

"It wasn't a natural one. I put it to you, sir, a woman twenty years older, and a lady . . ."

"No doubt you had your own reasons. But there had been frequent dissensions over money?"

"She hated to part, if that's what you mean. I

believe she'd sooner have seen me taken for owing money than paid, if she didn't think she was getting enough in return."

CHAPTER VIII

THE other members of the family had a far less grilling time. Norman was accustomed to coroners' courts and knew the kind of thing to say. His was not, perhaps, an altogether enviable position. The will had disclosed the fact that he benefited to the value of fifteen thousand pounds. He acknowledged that, but added it had come to him as a considerable surprise.

"Mrs. John had not given you any reason for supposing she would leave you such an amount?"

"Oh, well, I honestly don't know the answer to that. She had surprised me the last time I was at Aston Merry by showing a good deal of sympathy with my aims, asking me how much money I should need, and listening with apparent interest to quite a lot of professional data and incident. Of course, I shouldn't have expected her to leave me an amount like fifteen thousand. In fact, considering the way she knew I'd dispose of it, I call it princely."

"Quite. And did you refer to your work during your conversation with her on the last day of her life?"

"Yes. Among a number of other things."

"And isn't it a fact that after your last interview she sent for her lawyer?"

"I believe it is."

"Does that suggest anything to you?"

"She may have wished to increase my inheritance."

"Did you think that probable?"

"With a woman like my grandmother, it's impossible ever to guess what she's going to do. But on the whole, no, I shouldn't have been surprised if she had increased it."

"What makes you say that?"

"We'd been talking about past days; we spoke of my father, and how she'd never been able to see the magnificence of the thing he'd done. And how she had refused to help us then. It's true she said nothing tangible, but I think she may have meant to increase the amount."

"You are what's called optimistic, Dr. Bell?"

"I am at the moment a witness endeavouring to give you the information you want," said Norman coolly.

There was that about his composure that seemed to shake the coroner; he asked no more questions, and Norman retired as unruffled as he had appeared. But after he had gone there were whispers between the fur tippets and others to the effect that there went a fanatic, and it was easy for a doctor to lay hands on drugs.

Neville had only asked this witness one question, which was to the effect that he understood Norman had never seen the will and couldn't therefore know if Mrs. Wolfe had left him a legacy. "I gather from Mr. Nicholls that no one has ever seen it," Norman replied, "not even Wolfe himself. She seems to have made a corner in secrecy."

Rose in her turn admitted that she had had a disagreement with her grandmother the previous night, and that she didn't expect to benefit.

"On account of the disagreement?"

"Yes. Up till then she had meant to leave me something."

"You were convinced that she had altered her mind?"

"Oh, yes."

"That was disastrous for you?"

"Well, not disastrous, because we never knew how long she might go on. She might have lasted another twenty years. But it's nice to feel there's something coming one day."

"Yes. I believe, Miss John, you had some hope of raising a loan from your grandmother when you arrived at Aston Merry?"

"I had it in mind. I don't suppose I should ever have had the courage to make the suggestion."

"And, of course you realised, after the conversation referred to, that such a thing would be out of the question?"

"Oh, yes." She acknowledged that she was in debt, though not seriously so, and said she hadn't seen her grandmother after her retirement.

"She wasn't the sort of old lady who likes you to go in and say good-night," she pointed out gravely.

The coroner treated this as flippancy and therefore deplorable.

"Now, I understand you are a woman journalist?" he continued in stern tones.

"Yes."

" You have recently written a series of articles in the *R*—— on vices of society ? "

Rose grinned and a dimple appeared in her blooming cheek. " Yes."

" Those were written at first-hand ? "

" What does that mean ? "

" I mean, you purport to describe various orgies in night clubs and places of that description. You had actually visited the clubs in question."

" Oh, yes."

" You say in one of your articles that the practice of taking drugs is more widely spread than any outsider imagines. You mention morphine."

" It's one of three most used."

" And the others are ? "

" Cocaine and opium."

" You weren't alarmed at the prospect of going to such places ? I understand you went unaccompanied."

Rose stared. " Of course not. It was my job."

" Now, Miss John, can you tell us if you have ever actually seen drugs passed in these clubs ? "

Rose turned and stared at Neville. " Do I have to answer that ? " she said.

" And what is your objection ? " A nasty old man, the coroner, with a voice as smooth as a banana skin.

" If it gets about that I talk too much, give people a chance of putting names to places, I shan't get these jobs."

" And that would distress you very much ? "

Rose said impatiently, " It's my living."

"The court may think it a rather deplorable way for a young girl to earn her bread."

"Is that slanderous?" Rose demanded of Neville. Like her mother, she had no sense of fitness. "Because, if it comes to that, lots of most eminent people make their living out of vice. Judges, you know, and barristers, and . . ."

"This is a coroner's court, not a young woman's drawing-room," observed the coroner with heavy sarcasm. "I must ask you to answer my question, Miss John. Did you ever actually see drugs passed?"

"Yes."

"It would have been possible for you to obtain drugs yourself?"

"You need money."

"But assuming that you had the money?"

"Oh, yes."

"Did you ever, for any reason, do so?"

"No. When you've seen what it does to other people, you aren't very keen to join them."

"I see," The coroner's voice was openly disapproving. "Now, Miss John, can you tell the jury where you were on the evening of Tuesday between nine and ten p.m.?"

"In the billiard-room with my cousin, Anthony."

"The whole of that time?"

"Longer than that, I think."

"Just the pair of you?"

"Yes. Margaret, the servant, came in once to ask if we'd have cocoa. So delightfully rural, we thought."

"You didn't leave the room at all during that time? Think carefully before you reply."

" I don't need to think. I know I didn't. It was much too absorbing. I don't often get the chance of playing with any one as skilled as my cousin."

On the whole, he didn't get much change out of Rose. Still he had managed to raise a doubt in the jury's mind. Neville had no questions to ask her. He did not think she was one of the people who needed defending. It would take the police all their time to show that she had access to the old woman's room or the means to achieve murder.

Anthony corroborated Rose's evidence. He said he knew very little about morphine, and none of his friends was addicted to its use. He had had no hopes from his grandmother's will, and, in fact, he understood from Mr. Nicholls that his name was only mentioned to explain the old lady's reasons for cutting him out completely. He hadn't been particularly surprised to hear of her death ; he knew very little about medicine, but he understood that people who went up and down as rapidly as his grandmother did might collapse at any time.

Then it was Derek's turn. He agreed that he was engaged to marry his cousin, and that he hoped to do so in the near future. He had no private means, nor had she, but he had hopes of success in his own calling. After all, he pointed out gravely, hope was part of a man's assets when it came to totalling his income.

" But you were aware that it was Mrs. Wolfe's intention to leave her granddaughter the bulk of her fortune ? "

" She'd always said so, but, of course, you couldn't

count on things with any one so temperamental as she was."

"Did you think you personally would receive a legacy?"

"I was quite sure I shouldn't. My grandmother disliked both my parents. And when I heard I came into five thousand pounds, I was amazed."

"A very pleasant source of amazement. Now, Mr. Blake, on the night of the 25th October, between, say, nine-fifteen and ten o'clock, where were you?"

"About nine-fifteen I was talking to Miss Carol John in the hall. About a quarter to ten the doctor went, and my cousin said she must settle our grandmother for the night. She filled the syringe and went into the sick-room. I hung about waiting for her, thinking she wouldn't be long. As a matter of fact she was twenty minutes."

"And where were you during this time?"

"I waited about in the passage."

"Near Miss Carol's room?"

"Yes."

"So that if any one had entered the room, you must have seen them?"

"Unquestionably."

"And you saw no one?"

"No one."

"Now, do you remember noticing the morphia phial in Miss Carol's room? Or didn't you actually see it?"

"Yes. I saw her fill it. There was a good deal in the phial and I remember thinking how queer it was to reflect that death lurked in that innocent-looking stuff."

" You thought it was innocent ? "

" It looked to me like water."

Neville drew a sharp breath ; he felt he'd like to knock Derek's head against a wall.

" You wouldn't have known it wasn't water ? "

" Oh, no. I'm not a doctor."

" So if the phial had been filled with water, you'd have been none the wiser ? "

" There wouldn't be much point in charging the syringe with water," asid Derek, reasonably. " And anyway, there was a lot left after the syringe was charged."

" You observed it very closely ? "

" No. But one gets into the habit of noticing details. That's all."

" Still, you couldn't say that the phial was full of morphia when you saw Miss John charge it ? You admit it might have been water."

" I suppose it might. But you can't poison people with water. I don't see what you're driving at."

" I don't think that's relevant, Mr. Blake. Now, will you tell the jury what happened when Miss John first came out of the sick-room, after the doctor's arrival. You had some conversation. What did she say ? "

Derek's account tallied with Carol's, and there was nothing new to be learned here. But the coroner was like the inquisitive worm who wanted to know whether by boring deeply enough he'd reach Australia. The coroner meant to reach the truth, a much more hazardous destination. Nevertheless, he couldn't elicit anything fresh. Yet, as Derek left the court, Neville had an uncomfortable suspicion that the situation was worse than it had been ten minutes earlier.

Margaret Grant was the last witness of importance to be called. She openly cherished much animosity towards the family of her late employer, differing little in her regard towards any particular member. She said flatly that Wolfe only existed to see how much he could get out of his wife, and added she'd heard plenty of talk in the village in her time.

The coroner interrupted drily, "You are not here to repeat rumours or in fact to deal with any incident outside the scope of this court. We are here to determine, in so far as that is possible, the means and manner in which Mrs. Wolfe met her death. If you have any definite relevant information, that's another matter."

Margaret Grant looked sullen but resolute. In every word she spoke she betrayed her secret bitterness against every member of the family. She said darkly that every one knew that Mrs. Wolfe's money kept more people than herself and her husband, but collapsed when she was called to order and asked for chapter and verse.

Coming to the day before Mrs. Wolfe's death she said darkly that Dr. Bell had spent a powerful time that evening in the dead woman's room, and had angered her greatly, though she couldn't say how; but after he had gone Mrs. Wolfe decided to summon her man of affairs. She could repeat nothing of the conversation and when, later, Norman was recalled, he said coolly that he and his grandmother had discussed certain aspects of their earlier relationship, and had differed on certain points. But he offered no details, and was soon allowed to stand down. That, however, came afterwards. Continuing her evidence, Margaret said that on the night before Mrs. Wolfe was found poisoned she had been going downstairs from putting the tray outside Mrs. Wolfe's door, and had seen Miss John leave the sick-room and go down to the hall. Here she was presently joined by Mr. Blake, and the two embarked on a highly indiscreet conversation regarding their grandmother. Mr. Blake had said he thought the old devil was never going to let her (Carol) go, and Miss John had agreed that " she was in one of her most trying moods." She added that she had to give her the invalid food and the morphia, and then she'd be free for the night. Mr. Blake said he wished to God the old lady would die and get it over.

" You're quite certain—you are giving evidence on oath, remember—that that is what Mr. Blake said ? "

" As sure as I'm standing here. And Miss John said walls had ears, and she had some bad news anyhow ; she was going to be cut out of the will, and the lawyer was coming in the morning."

The court, that had been hovering in an ecstasy of indecision as to the true culprit, since Wolfe's evidence, now began slowly but steadily to revert to its original belief that Carol was the actual murderer ; some of them thought that foreign-looking cousin of hers was in it with her.

" What did Mr. Blake say ? "

" He said she'd change her mind in the morning, but Miss John said she didn't think so, not this time. And Mr. Blake said, 'Well, cheer up, perhaps she'd die in the night.' "

"You are quite sure of your evidence there, witness? Remember, this is a very serious position in which you are testifying and a word quoted wrongly may alter the whole meaning of a phrase."

"I'm altogether sure, sir," said Margaret, stubbornly. And nothing could shake her.

Neville lounged to his feet again. "You must have been quite close to hear all that conversation," he suggested.

"I was coming up the basement stairs with some silver I'd washed."

"You climb stairs very slowly, perhaps?"

"I've as much right to be tired as most at the end of my day," she retorted indignantly.

"Oh, quite. But you're sure that's all you heard?"

"That's all.'

"You didn't hear Miss John say that perhaps Mrs. Wolfe would make you her chief legatee?"

"I did not. And if I had, I'd have wanted her above all things to go on livin'. It's no use you trying to fix this on me."

"I wasn't trying to," said Neville truthfully. "Still, you didn't hear that?"

"I did not."

"You knew, I expect, that Mrs. Wolfe would leave you provided for?"

"She was a lady of her word to me, for all her husband was trying to get her to change her mind."

Neville looked astounded. "You don't mean he wanted her to change her mind in this connection?"

" Mr. Wolfe wouldn't think a servant had any rights."

" But, of course, there was no possibility of his succeeding ? "

" It's to be hoped not."

" You never had any reason to suspect that he might prevail on his wife."

" You can never be sure. And then I had heard the lawyer was coming the next day."

" And that might have meant, if Mr. Wolfe were successful, you'd be left unprovided for."

" You can never be sure," she repeated stubbornly.

" Quite right. As a lawyer I can back you up there. Old ladies take the most peculiar fancies. Of course it was important to you that Mrs. Wolfe shouldn't change her will in that direction. You probably haven't been able to save much ? "

" Not on the wages she pays," retorted Margaret grimly, " but then she always said she was going to make that right."

" I quite understand."

"And now it seems she was going to put me in for a bit more."

" Still, you didn't know that."

" No."

" And of course you had no reason to feel jealous, shall we say, about Miss John ? "

" I don't understand you."

Neville explained. " Well, if you had heard her say that Mrs. Wolfe intended to leave the bulk of her fortune to you and then before she could alter her will she died in rather mysterious circumstances, you might feel—shall we say aggrieved—that some one had prevented putting her generous schemes into action. But if you didn't know, of course you had no ground for any feeling against Miss John. You wouldn't wish to do her any sort of injury in the evidence you might give?"

Margaret Grant looked at him suspiciously and said nothing. The coroner said, "I think the form of your question is an improper one, Mr. Neville," and Neville bowed and sat down, thinking, "Of course it was. How else was I going to get my point into the thick heads of the jury?"

The police had a surprise to spring on the court, and one unpleasant enough in all the circumstances for the family of the dead woman.

"Miss Pamela Smythe."

Miss Smythe was a negligible, keenly-excited woman in the early thirties, dressed in the rather good suburban taste that is not, however, London's choice. You could just see the sort of house that went with that neat brown coat and skirt, the "good" straw hat, quite plain and set slightly aslant on the carefully waved hair, the sensible shoes, the wear-clean gloves, the well-kept handbag, a woman whose life was blameless and open to the day, a book that no one could conceivably wish to read.

Her voice was pleasant, but she spoke a little quickly. This was her first experience of an inquest, for in Havers Green it wasn't considered nice to be interested in possible crime to the extent of actually going to see the protagonists; you read about it in the press, and agreed sedately that it was terrible what people would do for money; and said in palliation that of course these younger folk hadn't been brought up to the stability of their elders, lest you be branded a censorious busybody.

Miss Smythe said, "On the 20th October—a Thursday—I was dining with some friends—that is, our hostess was the friend of my friend, and I happened to be with her the night Mrs. Lucas met us and asked my friend and me to have dinner with her at her club. I had never been there before; my own club is the Pelican, very cosy, but of course not grand like the International. Of course, my friend and Mrs. Lucas had a good deal to say to one another; they knew the same people and that gave me time to look round me. And soon I was attracted by the people at the next table. Three men and a girl, and all so attractive, if you know what I mean. Not just nice-looking or anything of that sort, but—well, I think personality's the word. They were brimming over with it. There were lots of other people in the room, but I didn't notice any of them. I didn't even feel out of it—the conversation between my friend and Mrs. Lucas, I mean—as I'd been afraid I might. You know what they say about two and three. But I couldn't help hearing what this quartette were saying; the tables were rather close together and they were talking quite loud. First of all, they talked about food, and then they began to talk about the Archer Murder Case, that had just been decided. They wondered if you could ever justify murder, and then they got on to Murder as a subject. Now I've always been interested in records of crime. My father was a barrister and I expect I get it from him. Anyway there it is." She could picture the expressions, half-awed, half-horrified of her pleasant suburban friends when they read that ; not just heard it passed on, neighbourly gossip that most likely wasn't true, but something actually in the papers, that you couldn't doubt.

" And you overheard some of their conversation, Miss Smythe ? "

" I've explained that I couldn't help that. No one detests eavesdropping more than I do. I'm always telling my servants . . . However, as I say, I couldn't help it. And they did say some rather odd things. To begin with, they wondered if crime was ever justified, and one of them, the doctor, I think, said he didn't see in some cases what other solution there was, where people were poisoning other people's lives. And then they told him that it would be easy for him, because doctors had special chances, and he asked why a man should be expected to wreck his professional reputation by letting his patients die, because people did feel badly about things like that, even if you could show it wasn't your fault ; and he said that if he had to commit a murder he'd do something violent with a hammer or just his hands, because no one would expect a doctor to do that ; they'd think he had so many opportunities. And then they began to talk about murder generally, and it did strike me what a lot they all knew about crime. The doctor said there were any number of violent crimes where the murderer had never been discovered, and he reeled off a whole list. I don't remember them all; there were two women who'd been strangled in trains, and a girl in Yorkshire who'd been strangled with a stocking, and a girl found in a ditch, and quite a lot of women who'd been hit on the head, Kate Dungay and Jane Roberts and Jane Clousen and a woman called Camp—oh, and a number of others."

" And was that all ? "

" No. The red-headed one—I didn't know then that he was an actor—said he preferred poison; it was tidier and more artistic, but the others said it was more easily traced. He said there were ways, and then they began to talk of their grandmother. The dark one they called Derek said it was about time she had another attack, and what a good thing it was that when she was ill she liked her own granddaughter about her. Most people, he said, were suspicious, if they were rich and you weren't, in case you succumbed to temptation and just tipped them over the edge. Then the red-headed one said that she, the girl, needn't polish off their grandmother on his account because he didn't stand to get anything. And then they wondered how long she'd live, and they thought for years, just for the pleasure of keeping them waiting."

There was no doubt about it, this was the star witness of the afternoon. The brown fur tippets were talking so eagerly they were threatened with expulsion from the court; whispers flew from lip to lip; there was a muttered suggestion that this was a deep-laid scheme in which every cousin was involved.

Norman thought, "I wonder what that titbit of gossip is going to cost me during the next twelve months."

Neville thought, " It's U.P. with both of them, I should say. Anyway, there isn't a hope for the girl."

The coroner was pressing Miss Smythe for more particular details ; the position became increasingly worse. It wasn't possible, in the grim surroundings of this court, to reproduce the gay inconsequence with which, no doubt, the subject had been dealt with at the Club.

Before the jury left the court the foreman asked a question. " Is it absolutely certain that the morphia was injected ? Is it possible that it was given through the mouth ? "

The court stiffened to a fresh attention. Marshall was recalled. He said it was quite possible for the morphia to be given in the invalid food. The difficulty about cases like this one, he added, was that individual cases varied so enormously. Morphia given subcutaneously acts far quicker, as a rule, than morphia taken through the mouth ; but here again it's almost impossible to generalise. He had known cases where death took place within the hour, though the normal time required was from six to twelve hours. In reply to a further question, he said that the food would be prepared in the kitchen, and no further cooking or treatment of any kind would be necessary.

The jury then retired.

They seemed to be away an interminable time. People began to wonder audibly what was keeping them. Surely a blind man could see who was guilty. But the responsibility, as Neville murmured to Rose, was not theirs.

"Do you know how it's going?" she whispered back.

"I'm afraid so."

"Not Carol?"

Neville nodded grimly.

"But she didn't do it. You can't be condemned for what you haven't done."

"You can be accused of it, I'm afraid. It's up to us to see that a permanent injustice doesn't take place."

For the remainder of the time, until the jury returned, he waited, outwardly debonair and collected, inwardly glum, thinking over the position; he wondered if the family would consult him about the defence. He had not a shred of doubt as to how the verdict would go, so far as Carol was concerned; the only thing he wasn't sure about was how far Derek would be officially implicated; unofficially, he would be in it up to his neck.

It was pretty clever of the police, he reflected, to have unearthed that loquacious suburban spinster. Simply revelling, she'd been; probably never enjoyed herself so much in all her starved, respectable life. Perhaps, after all, it wasn't so clever of them, though; no doubt, the difficulty would have been to ignore her. She'd probably been tearing round with her tongue out, telling every one—but simply every one. It wasn't a chance you could expect her to miss.

At last the jury returned. There was an intense

hush all over the court as they resumed their seats. Now that the moment was upon them, Rose felt a choking sensation, a sudden dizziness. She put out a blind hand and Anthony caught it.

" Brace up. We can't afford casualties at this stage."

The solemn words rang out on the court's sultry air.

" Gentlemen are you all agreed ? "

" We are."

" And what is your verdict ? "

" We find that the deceased died from morphine poisoning, wilfully administered ; and we find Carol John guilty of administering the same."

Part II
THE CRIME

CHAPTER I

THE big dreary house at Aston Merry had been left to Wolfe and Dorothy John and the servant, Margaret Grant. Of the others, Carol had been charged before a magistrate and committed for trial for wilful murder, and her cousins and Rupert Neville had returned to town to face the job of establishing her innocence. For this purpose they were met in Derek's extravagant rooms in Adelphi.

" Before we begin," their host observed, " there's one thing I'm burning to know. Why didn't they take me as well as Car ? "

" They don't want to run the risk of arresting any one who may conceivably be innocent," Rupert explained. " If you were involved, or if the jury thinks you were, there'll be time enough to get hold of you later on. Meanwhile, you're as well at liberty ; you may not be able to do much—we don't know—but in prison you couldn't do anything at all."

Anthony grinned, " 'Ear, 'ear," he applauded. " Carry on, Rupert. What's our first step ? "

" Our defence has to adopt one of two courses," Neville told them. " Either we've got to say there isn't sufficient evidence to convict this girl, or even to let the case go to a jury or (if it actually gets as far as a formal verdict) we must rouse enough doubt in the minds of the twelve ladies and gentlemen concerned to prevent their returning an adverse verdict. That's one way of doing it, and not a very satisfactory way. It'll simply mean that suspicion will go on resting on Car and probably on you, Derek—I don't think any one else will be victimised; they couldn't show you had sufficient motive and opportunity."

"Don't you think it's quite possible Wolfe may have done it?"

"He may. And of course all this sleeping-draught affair may be a blind. He could have put morphia into the invalid food knowing the whole thing was going to be stirred up, so there'd be no fear of its settling in a sediment at the bottom of the cup and not being absorbed."

"In that case he'd have scattered a bit of the powder on the tray and got rid of the rest—that could lay the false trail."

"What's his motive?" asked Norman, lifting his fine brows. "Afraid he may be going to be cut out of the will?"

"His wife may have told him so."

"He didn't know the contents of the will the night before she died."

"Did he know the lawyer was coming?"

"Yes," said Anthony. "I told him myself. He hadn't known till then. At least, he said he hadn't, and I think he was genuine."

"What time was this?"

"On the Wednesday night."

"After he went down to the town, with you?" asked Norman.

"Yes. Just as we started."

"How did you know about the lawyer?" asked Neville.

"Aunt Dorothy let it out. I was talking to her for a few minutes while she was waiting for grandmother to send for her."

"That's rather against Wolfe, isn't it?" suggested Norman.

"Being so upset? We don't really know the cause of that."

"He said it made him feel a fool being excluded from his wife's affairs," contributed Anthony.

"That may quite well cover the cause of his discomfiture," Neville agreed. "You're sure he didn't know how the land lay?"

Norman nodded. "He wasn't acting when he was talking to me."

"Then perhaps after all he's not mixed up in the murder, he simply wanted that sleeping-draught to keep his wife quiet while he explored the room for her will. Did she keep it there, does any one know?"

No one did. "Dorothy might," Anthony suggested.

"My dear fellow, grandmother wouldn't tell Dorothy anything. She always treated the woman as if she were a half-wit."

"That might be the very reason she wouldn't think it mattered her knowing."

"Did Dorothy know the contents of the will?"

"She says not, and I should think that's right."

"What's the position at present?" asked Rose curiously. "Carol gets forty thousand pounds under the will, but if our defence fails——" she hesitated.

"If our defence fails, the question of her inheriting

won't be raised," said Neville brutally. "That's why we can't take any risks. I wonder if we could prove that Wolfe really was in his wife's room late that night."

"He was up at midnight taking rum," corroborated Derek, "because I met him. Looking as frightened as if he'd seen a ghost. I don't believe he really meant to have a drink either. It sounded to me like an excuse."

Neville jumped at that. "It probably was. Most likely he was going to his wife's room then. But he had to invent something when you unexpectedly side-tracked him. You didn't stay down with him? That's a pity."

"Meaning I could have seen where he went?"

"He'd hardly have let you do that. But you might have heard footsteps or something."

"Well, unfortunately I didn't stay. I left him looking hot and unhappy, combing back his beastly hair."

"Doing what?" exclaimed Neville and Anthony simultaneously, and Neville went on, "Don't you see, that's the evidence we've been looking for? If he had the comb at midnight, he couldn't have dropped it on Mrs. Wolfe's bed at half-past nine. Not that any one believes he does, of course. That gives us something definite to work on. After all, we don't want to get just a dubious acquittal. We want to pin down the criminal beyond all doubt. Otherwise, Carol will be pointed at, I won't say all her life, but for a good many years, as another of the successful murderers. As a matter of fact, this isn't nearly such a hopeless case as a good many others, because we've got quite a lot to work on. There are other suspects here . . ."

" But no one else who we know could get hold of morphia." That was Rose again, gloomy, deliberately unhelpful.

" We don't know. What you mean is that at the present moment we can't prove that any one else had morphia in his or her possession at the time of Mrs. Wolfe's death. But morphia can be obtained by all kinds of people, particularly in tablet form. You yourself, Rose, agreed that you'd seen morphia passed. Norman, here, as a doctor, can get all the morphia he wants. Probably Derek and Anthony," he smiled in a friendly way, " could lay hands on it if they really meant to, in spite of the evidence. The question is, did any one know that she would be having morphia ? " He looked at them keenly.

" Oh yes, she always does," said Derek immediately.

" She's had it before ? "

" Yes. This is the third—or is the fourth—fatal attack she's had when we've been sent for ? "

" Fourth," said Anthony.

" Well, she's had Carol every time.

" And morphia every time ? "

" Yes."

" And each time you've all gone down ? "

" Yes again."

" And Wolfe was always there, of course ? "

" He was."

" And the unmarried daughter ? "

" Yes once more."

"So that if any one meant to do away with the old lady it would be easy to decide on the means?"

"Except for Carol," insisted Norman. "Morphia is about the last thing she'd use, because it would turn attention to her at once. The thing doesn't make sense."

"You have to remember that, according to the prosecution, she only made up her mind on the spur of the minute. Up till then she'd been satisfied enough to wait. But when she saw she was going to lose the money she leapt at her one chance."

"Knowing she'd be accused at once?" insisted Norman. "It's absurd."

"She didn't expect any one to raise questions about the manner of death," Neville reminded him.

"Still, you're not dealing with a complete fool," broke out Derek. "She must know that if any question was raised she'd be the first person to be pointed at."

"If it was any one else, the crime must have been premeditated," Norman said. "If we could prove that any other member of the household had been in possession of morphia at that time, we should have the foundation of the defence."

"I think Norman's right," put in Rose. "It seems to me that if Car had been going to kill grandma she would have abstained from morphia as saints from mortal sin. There are other ways ..."

"Oh quite. But how many of them were open to her? You have to remember all the circumstances, her sex, her position, her comparative lack of weapons. So many of these violent crimes attract attention at once . . ."

"And so many don't," put in Norman grimly, "as we're already agreed. The trouble is, every one's getting too subtle these days."

"That's one of our disadvantages," Anthony chipped in. "D'you remember Barrie telling some actor that he wanted him to cross the stage from left to right, silently conveying that he had an aunt at Surbiton?"

"When you've quite finished theorising and being brilliant, perhaps we can come back to Car," suggested Derek, stonily. "It's established beyond a doubt that grandmother did die of morphine poisoning, and I agree with Norman that it's about the silliest weapon Car could use. But, of course, Rupert's right. The only thing that'll be effective will be for us to discover who the actual criminal is. I think we ought to begin by finding out whether any of the rest of us, bar Norman, whose profession helps him here, could actually get hold of morphia."

There was a moment's silence. Then Rose said in hesitant tones, "I suppose I could get it if I set my mind to it and had enough money. Done up in the hem of a handkerchief, or passed in a miniature bouquet—I've known it distributed in both those ways. And of course there are my articles, which I suppose might count as adverse evidence. But I've never actually had any or taken any."

"And I haven't either," agreed Anthony. "I'm not even sure if I could get hold of it. People talk as if the stage teemed with drug fiends only too eager to initiate you into their horrid practices, but

That superstition I should scout.
There is more faith in honest doubt
As Tennyson has pointed out
Than in those nasty creeds.

Actually I don't know any one who'd palm me any, though it's true that fellow Poynter—he's at the —— at the moment—does take it. He told me about it once, by way of warning, I gathered. Said he was having his hell here, though, when he goes on, he's only got to look at his audience, and there's a hush like the Last Day."

Derek said, "I honestly don't believe I could have got hold of any. You wouldn't give it me if I asked for it, would you, Norman?"

"Why should I risk my reputation for you?" asked Norman simply.

"Then Norman and Rose and you at a pinch," Neville nodded to Anthony, "might be able to lay hands on morphine. What about Wolfe and Miss Dorothy John?"

"Oh, hardly Dorothy," said Derek. "She'd be too much afraid."

"Don't lets take that sort of thing into consideration at present," Anthony suggested. "We're at point one still. Could she conceivably have got hold of it?"

"Could she have got at the phial?" Norman suggested.

"How, when it was kept locked up?"

"What kind of a lock was it?"

"Oh, just the ordinary sort you always find on dressing-tables."

"The kind that practically any one can pick, and that'll open to about a dozen keys. If there were locks anywhere else in the house, they were probably all the same kind. Oh, I think you could prove opportunity very easily for her. She's one of the few members of the household who wouldn't be hard put to it to make excuses if she were seen in Car's room; she could say she wanted something for her mother, or was looking for Car, or anything."

"But what about motive?" demanded Rose. "It's impossible to conceive of her as a murderess. Besides, why, when for five-and-twenty years, ever since she came of age, she's been grandmother's butt and victim without seeming to resent it much, should she suddenly break out into skilful crime? Because it is skilful. I don't believe she's capable of it. She's too much of a nonentity."

"Hardly that," Neville reasoned. "You've admitted yourself she's kept going under most unfavourable circumstances for a quarter of a century. And she's neither a nervous wreck nor, physically, hopelessly incapacitated. No one capable of that staying power can be altogether negligible. There must be something—some ambition, some affection, some passion even, that supplies her with fuel. A woman like that's capable of a great deal. And not having any one to confide in, she's kept all that feeling smouldering for years. As for why she should choose this particular time, we all have our breaking-point. And we don't know what her relations with her mother actually were a week ago. They may have been at daggers drawn."

"Would she try and involve Car, though?" asked Anthony, deeply shocked. "That takes a lot of swallowing."

"It's the very reason why I'm inclined to suspect her," countered Neville warmly. "If she had a right to detest any one, it was Car. She's the daughter of the house, she has to put up with a woman like Mrs. Wolfe day in, day out, for years, she gets no thanks and no fun. But whenever a crisis arises, Carol's sent for. Carol's consulted, Carol has authority. Miss John's nowhere. Every one in the house sees her humiliation. Carol's even proclaimed the old lady's heir. Mrs. Wolfe remarks largely whenever the mood takes her, regardless of her audience, that she isn't going to see her money squandered on High Church societies; the daughter will get a pittance to keep her alive. If ever you had a case where jealousy might be suspected, and white-hot jealousy at that, here it is. Besides, a woman living that secluded life would brood on trifles that more normal people wouldn't trouble their heads about; her mother's scathing tongue may have done more harm than anybody's guessed. And then, having nothing particular to occupy her mind, Miss John could scheme till the last detail reached perfection. She'd know the ways of the household, know about the invalid food being prepared at a certain hour, know about the doctor's second visit, even know that it was the servant's habit to wash the cup overnight, so no trace would remain. She wouldn't take so many chances as any one else. She can't account for her time definitely between nine and ten. Part of the time she was with her mother, she says. She doesn't wear a watch; she can't be certain; she would not like to perjure herself."

"And she wouldn't need a second supply of morphia," exclaimed Derek. "That simplifies matters a lot. But how in the world do we prove a thing like that?"

"We don't. We're going to have an expert in on this. Personally, I don't believe in the perfect murder, anyway not when it's planned. If you've made a plan, even if you think you've destroyed all the clues, still you've trodden a certain path, and other people may discover the direction. If you kill some one without premeditation, you may just escape, if your luck's in. It's the safer way, if you must commit violent crime."

"Like Lord Arthur Savile," murmured Anthony, and Derek continued, "I appreciate your remark that this isn't really such a difficult case. It appears to me simply to bristle with improbabilities."

"We'll go on," said Neville, unmoved. "There's Wolfe. Now he's been behaving in a very suspicious manner from the first. He may have put up all this blarney about the sleeping-draught in order to attract attention to the tablets; it seems a bit odd that a man of his age, who isn't completely a fool, should go out of his way to consult you, Norman, about a draught, when what you'd expect him to do would be to ask a chemist. That looks to me a if he expected questions to be asked later—did he make a lot of fuss about secrecy?"

Norman nodded.

"That's unnatural again. There's nothing criminal about taking a sleeping-draught. You see my point. No one would have identified the tablets with him, if he hadn't drawn attention to them. He'd argue that if he were going to give his wife morphine, no one would expect him to give her the sleeping-draught as well ; so when it's proved absolutely that he gave her the sleeping-draught, he'd suppose that would absolve him from any other accusation."

"And why did he go into her room, if he knew she'd be dead ?" Rose asked.

"He was probably terrified of a hitch. These amateur criminals contrive six times out of ten to give themselves away through sheer funk. He might think she hadn't taken the invalid food, and it would be damning if what was left did happen to be analysed.

"It was unfortunate that the cup had been washed overnight. Perhaps he thought the stuff hadn't had any effect on her ; or perhaps he did really want something. But that I think unlikely. But he may have wanted to put up the bluff that he was searching for something and left the comb there on purpose. Then suspicion would be roused against him, and would be dispersed almost at once because if he really had killed his wife, he could afford to wait for what was coming to him—in a purely material way, I mean, and there'd be no point in his searching her room. No, I think he plotted it all out very neatly."

"Then we've marked him down as the real criminal ?"

"I wouldn't like to speak so certainly as that. But I think he may very probably prove to be our man."

"We're supposing that the morphine was put into the food, aren't we?" meditated Anthony. "That does narrow the field. Because the stuff only stood outside the door for half-an-hour, according to Margaret."

"But we have found no one who admits to being anywhere near it during that time, which means that any one may have been. You and Rose seem to be cleared, but practically every one else at a pinch could be implicated."

"At present," said Derek drily, "we don't seem to have a case at all. We're trying to build up something against Wolfe. We believe he drugged his wife, but we can't prove yet that he poisoned her. That apparently is our job."

"You don't mean that literally, I suppose," remarked Neville, "because, if you have got any picturesque ideas in your mind of doing your own sleuthing, you can abandon them. For one thing, this is much too serious a case for us to take any risks, and it stands to reason the expert will be more efficient than any of us can hope to be. For another, if you'll forgive my being candid, until we get a definite verdict, practically every member of the household at Aston Merry is suspect, and must be given an opportunity of laying false clues or building up a sound personal defence. And thirdly, even if you were all as innocent as angels and everybody knew it, you're much too well known in the neighbourhood to be a scrap of use at this job. I know Anthony's dying to put on a beard and smoked glasses, and go down as a foreign visitor, but it's no use. We can't afford to throw away a single shot in the locker. I know a very good man, a chap called Gordon, and I'll go along and see him this afternoon. Now, before we break up, there are still some points to consider. The servant, Margaret Grant, for instance. I think she might be included in our list of suspects. The money motive would hold good in her case, too."

"But she knew she was coming into the annuity eventually. Would she have taken such a chance?" Norman wanted to know. "And would she have the technical knowledge? I suppose she could have got at the morphia as easily as Aunt Dorothy. She'd know about locks, and whether there'd been a locksmith at the house lately; it wouldn't look odd if she were seen in Carol's room. She'd have more opportunity than any one, because she mixed the invalid food, and if by any chance it hadn't been drunk, she could have thrown the contents of the cup away and no one would have been any the wiser."

"She'd only get the money provided she was still in grandmother's service at the time of grandmother's death," added Rose acutely. "I know all about speaking ill of the dead, but I don't believe myself there was much love lost between grandmother and Margaret. I believe they fought like cats. It wouldn't surprise me a bit to know that grandmother was fooling Margaret all along the line and meant to sack her just before the end and get the last laugh. I know it's a vile thing to say, but grandmother did do vile things."

"And Margaret may have realised that?"

"Grandmother may actually have given her

notice, for all we know. No one would have told us."

"She was with your grandmother on the last afternoon?"

"Yes. She and Car and Aunt Dorothy took alternative watches in the sick-room. She was madly jealous of Car, you know. Not of Aunt Dorothy. Nobody could be jealous of her."

"So there's a double motive. Jealousy of your cousin and fear of losing her own legacy. She may have had her own reasons as to why Nicholls had been summoned. Let's see. She was to have two hundred a year. The motive must have been money, I think, whoever's guilty."

"I suppose so. That rules you out," Derek shot his head in Anthony's direction, "but the rest of us—Carol stood to get forty thousand pounds, Margaret and I five thousand pounds, Dorothy the same, grandmother saying she'd only give away any surplus or waste it, five thousand to Rose, and the balance, after paying legacies, etc., to Wolfe, together with the house and furniture, with the proviso that he lost everything if he married again."

"I wouldn't be surprised to hear he had a lady friend in the neighbourhood," said Rose, inelegantly. "He isn't the celibate type, and he and grandmother have only seen one another across the breakfast-table for years now."

Neville wondered dispassionately whether Philip John had ever regretted his rash second marriage, or if its racy idiom had appealed to him after the refinement of his earlier married life.

"You read too many novels from the Free

Library," Anthony told Rose affectionately. " No need for there to be a woman in it."

" Why else would he want the money ? There's only two reasons men get driven to murder, this sort, I mean, not the kind where a fellow suddenly loses his head and socks the lady with the kitchen poker. One of them is if he's running a business and he's got to have money or else everything'll crash down on him. Well, Wolfe wasn't doing that. He hasn't got the brains. And the other is if he's got in a mess over a woman. No, let me finish. I don't mean he'd do grandmother in and take all that chance just because he was sick of her and wanted something a bit younger and softer. But suppose he'd got a girl into trouble, and they wanted money ? You know 'swell's I do grandmother wouldn't give him sixpence without wanting a receipt."

" And she has to countersign all his cheques. That's true. But couldn't he put the girl off a bit, seeing every one expected the old lady to die ? "

" Maybe he could. But look here. Suppose the old lady's found out ? Suppose she tells him she's going to cut him right out of the will ? She would, you know. She never treated him like a proper husband, not much after the start anyway, but she kept his head in blinkers, and if he started to look round them at any pretty face or nice pair of legs I'll bet she docked his pocket-money for a month to come."

" Let's get this straight," said Neville. " You think your grandmother found out about Wolfe. But when ? She didn't have much chance the last day or two, because she was too ill. I suppose she didn't get any letters. We could find that out for certain from Carol. And, if she'd known beforehand, surely she'd have sent for Nicholls straight away."

"Perhaps finding out was what gave her the fit. And directly she got a bit better she sent for Nicholls."

Norman was following up his own train of thought. "I wonder if Wolfe could have known Carol was going out that evening?" he speculated, "and leaving the coast clear for him. She'd never tell him, of course. But who might know?"

"Didn't she and Derek arrange it in the hall? They might have been overheard."

"But by whom?"

"I've got it," Derek exclaimed. "Margaret Grant."

"And I've got it, too," shouted Rose, interrupting him in her excitement. "Suppose she's the woman we're after, the woman Wolfe's carrying on with?"

She looked round enthusiastically, but Neville only said in dry tones, "It might be as well first of all to establish this legendary liaison, don't you think?"

Derek said a little grudgingly, "You must admit, Rupert, that it would fit in. And suppose grandmother had found out? They could work the thing perfectly between them. There'd be no fear in Margaret's mind of Wolfe ever giving her away. He wouldn't dare. It would involve himself too much. And Margaret's got him in her power for ever. She'd love a position like that."

"I've remembered something else," said Rose.

"Some time ago, the last time Car was down at Aston Merry, Marshall told her he wanted to get rid of Margaret, but nothing happened. Wolfe stopped him."

"Wolfe?"

"Yes. He said she'd been there a dozen years, and in these days in the country servants were difficult to get, and I daresay he implied that grandmother wasn't very easy to live with. But there may have been a double motive."

They continued the discussion for some time, and then the meeting broke up. Norman had an appointment, and Rose was collecting opinions from various young society mothers for a symposium on "Motherhood and Modern Marriage." Derek and Anthony went off together, and Neville went to see Gordon.

"Do tell me," asked Anthony, genuinely intrigued, as he and Rose walked back together, "Is Hattie frightfully thrilled about all this?"

"If it weren't Car, she'd be loving it. After all, you can't expect her to care much about grandmother."

"Since we're being candid, none of us care much about grandmother."

"That's true. Still, though I didn't particularly want her to live—she was selfish and a nuisance—I didn't want her to die in this spectacular manner and get Car arrested for her murder. If only it weren't Car."

He walked along for a minute in silence. Then, slipping his arm through hers, he said, "It's no use, Rosie. You're only kicking against the pricks, and you aren't getting any change out of it either, anyhow, it wouldn't have worked, if Car had gone into a convent and Derek had never set eyes on her. He's too much of a gent for folk like you and me."

CHAPTER II

I

GORDON had, of course, read the case and found it, he said, absorbing. It was the kind of position he liked. Straightforward work was always apt to bore him a little, but this tangle of motive and opportunity, and the psychological reactions implicit in the crime intrigued him more than he could explain. Together he and Neville debated the points that had already been made at the morning's meeting, and then went on to discuss the position of the members of the family.

"Beginning with Norman Bell," suggested Neville. "Can we put him right out of the picture? It would be easy for him to provide himself with morphia, he'd be at home with the technical side of it, he'd know exactly when to administer it and how, and what to expect. And you can supply motive with very little difficulty. No one actually knows what took place between his grandmother and himself on that morning. If she was going to disinherit him and make his cherished plans an utter impossibility, I think he's fanatic enough to consider any means worth the end."

"Even getting this girl involved?"

"His father was one of the martyrs of science, and he probably doesn't regard the individual life very gravely. He wouldn't think that two lives to secure so much was too heavy a price. And he certainly wouldn't dare take chances with so much at stake."

"Being a doctor himself, he'd expect Marshall to be suspicious, I suppose? Otherwise, why call attention to the dead woman's eyes? Marshall might have passed the whole thing over as death from natural causes."

"I doubt it. There was already the question of the comb. He knew Marshall was going to ask questions, and then it might be difficult to explain why a man of his experience had been so guileless. Oh, I don't think he was taking any chances. In a sense, for all his humanity, he's cold-blooded. He's a scientist first and foremost. I put that suggestion forward for what it's worth. I'm leaving the actual work to you."

Gordon, who had made an indecipherable note or two on a slip of paper, said, "And the rest? This man Blake, for instance?"

"Thing's don't look too rosy for him, and that's a fact. He's known to be badly in debt. In fact, he's in the hands of the Jews. He admittedly doesn't know where to turn for money. As soon as his grandmother dies, he virtually comes into forty thousand pounds, since he and Carol are going to be married at the first opportunity. According to himself, he knew nothing about the five thousand he was going to inherit, and I doubt if we shall be able to prove anything one way or the other about that. He had several days' notice in which to prepare his plans; he was on the spot when Miss John—Carol,

I mean—gets the message. He knows, as every one in the household knows, that when she has these attacks, she has morphia. He may even know about the evening drink. Provided he can lay hands on the poison, he's got both motive and opportunity. What I can't square is his filling up Car's morphia tube with water. That meant his losing the whole forty thousand."

"But suppose, as you say, he knew about the five thousand? That might be enough to save his bacon; and it's better to lose forty thousand pounds than your life."

"Assuming that he knew about his own legacy. But if he'd left the phial untouched, his cousin would be secure, and it would be up to the police to prove where the morphia had come from. Of course, it might be traced to him. . . ."

"Besides, there's another point. He may have used that morphia because there was no way he could lay hands on any other."

"And the plan wasn't premeditated. Not before he came to Aston Merry, I mean."

"He may have been sure his grandmother was going to die, and when he saw it was another false alarm, knowing his own desperation, he stole the morphia, and hoped the substitution would never be noticed."

"Another point. What opportunity was there for any one to tamper with the phial during the short time that it was admittedly left unguarded? Derek says he was in the passage the whole time, and would have seen any one approach . . ."

"But that is probably inaccurate. According to

the papers, he met his cousin in the hall wearing a hat and coat. He must have left the passage for a minute or two to fetch these. I understand he sleeps upstairs. So that for a moment or so the passage would be unguarded. The work would not take a minute, probably. Daring? But the whole crime's remarkably daring."

"That seems to spread suspicion to every one in the house."

"Not quite every one," said Gordon. "For instance, I think the two cousins, Anthony and Rose, who were playing billiards during the whole of the time that the invalid food stood outside the door, might be acquitted. They really hadn't any opportunity of tampering with the stuff, either before it left the kitchen or afterwards. And the girl they call Alethea, who helps in the kitchen, has a cleft palate and is half-witted, might be ruled out, too, I think."

They continued discussing ways and means for the greater part of the afternoon. At last Gordon said, "Our chorus to-day seems to be, 'Nothing happened, so far as we know.' The position will look a lot clearer when we have a little definite information on various points. The first thing to do is discover who else, besides Bell, could have got at an independent supply of morphia."

"Of course, morphia's available wherever there are doctors and chemists, but it's not at all easy to get hold of. It might be worth trying the various chemists in the neighbourhood of Aston Merry and see if any attempts have been made recently by members of the household to lay hands on morphia.

That shouldn't be difficult. I think I'd better start with those inquiries, that I can do quite openly, and then I'll hang about as a casual visitor and see what gossip I can pick up."

II

It was not difficult to discover that no chemist in the Aston Merry district had dispensed morphia to any member of the household at the End House during the past few weeks, nor had any one answering to the description of either Wolfe or Margaret attempted to obtain morphia by illicit means.

Marshall, with whom Gordon talked matters over during that first visit, said eagerly, " So that's the line of the defence, is it ? Well, all luck to you—though that may be a hard thing to say, considering what a rough deal this fellow's had. But I don't think you'll pull it off."

" No ? " murmured Gordon.

" No. I don't think he's got the pluck. Not unless he were absolutely driven."

" Meaning if he were more alarmed by some other contingency than by the chance of being taken for murder ? "

" Precisely—if there is such a thing. But anyway he's a fellow who plays for safety."

To satisfy Gordon he formally examined his stock of morphia and assured him it had not been tampered with. " But there are other sources," Gordon told himself, walking back to the station. " Chemists are careful men, but even they get bamboozled sometimes," and he recalled a case several years earlier when a pretty young woman had, by a ruse, obtained sufficient antimony to poison her elderly husband and his suspicious sister.

He followed up his intention of going down to Aston Merry a second time, incognito. The public was slow to recognise the difference between private detectives and the police, regarding them as inter-related, rather like the private and public wards of a hospital. You paid for one, and presumably got more individual attention, but you couldn't separate the two.

III

So the following evening a plumpish, shortish man, dark-complexioned and dark-eyed, appeared in the little village of Aston Merry, where he engaged a room at the inn. He gave his name as Mr. Felix Michael, and said he was the representative of a large London firm. His voice was slightly but not un-pleasantly accented, and he made himself very affable to Mr. Bowie. His business, he explained, was photography. He had brought a professional-looking camera down with him, and his intention was to get commissions in the neighbourhood.

"Won't be much doing here," said Bowie dubiously.

"There is no obligation," the stranger explained. "Just let us take the picture, then if you like it you pay, if not—not." He spread his hands in an un-English gesture.

"What's the game ?" asked the landlord bluntly.

Mr. Michael smiled. "I will explain. It is no use to do this kind of thing in the big towns ; there are too many studios, too much competition. But here there is so little, and I dare say the people here are as vain as they are elsewhere, and if they see a nice picture of themselves or their little children they will be tempted to buy. Or perhaps there are ladies and gentlemen here who let their houses, and would like a photograph to put in an advertisement. I have had much experience of this kind of work," continued Mr. Michael, with blissful inaccuracy, " and always I have been successful. We are not expensive like the big shops, and we have no big rents to pay ; we can afford to be cheap."

Mr. Bowie thought, " Why the hell do we let these dagoes get away with it ? Why didn't some chap round here think of photographs ? " Because he knew that the fellow would get commissions. It was a neighbourhood that hadn't yet subscribed to the modern ways of thought, and babies were frequently born here, too frequently, often, to please their parents ; and young folk got married and though there was a fellow who came over and took pictures, he was very costly, and this chap might do quite well. Had the gift of the gab, too.

The next morning Mr. Michael started on his round. He didn't go too early ; he didn't want to upset the housewives by making them answer the door when they were busy. He started, in fact, on the shops. He went into the chemist's. The chemist said : No, thanks, he didn't want any this morning.

" You do not pay anything," Mr. Michael insisted. " You let me take your picture or your shop, and if you do not like it you do not pay."

The chemist looked sceptical. That wasn't the way business was done.

"Where's the catch?" he asked inelegantly, lounging over his counter.

"There is not one." The foreigner was very reassuring.

"Well," the chemist did a little gesturing on his own account, "I can't stop you taking a picture of my shop, can I?"

The stranger smiled; he set up his camera; he fussed and fidgeted; he attracted a lot of attention; a lady who was buying some cold cream asked Mr. Whirter what it was all about.

"You better ask him. He wants to take the picture, and if I like it I can buy it. Can't say fairer than that."

A little crowd had collected round Mr. Michael. His camera was very striking; it seemed an awe-inspiring apparatus to be used for anything so simple as photographing a village shop.

"What made him pick on you, I wonder?" said the tobacconist, in some jealousy.

Mr. Whirter said nothing.

"Working through the village from top to bottom," suggested the village wag with a grin.

The tobacconist looked angry; he was a richer man than any one guessed, much richer than the chemist. The stranger was occupied with his camera. He reappeared from behind it for a moment, looking agitated.

"If you will please stand back," he said. They stood back obligingly. They didn't get many excitements in this little place. They talked in animated tones one to another; the man behind the camera strained his ears to catch a mention of the Wolfe poisoning case. He couldn't very well, he decided, open the matter up himself. But presently, after a little patience, his chance came. Some one was chaffing the chemist.

"He'll be looking for his photograph in the paper before long," the woman called. "First the police all over the shop asking questions about poison, and then . . ."

A second member of the crowd took up the cry. "That's why, of course. I bet this fellow's only a journalist. Wants a picture of Mr. Whirter for the London papers, and gets one by a trick." (For Mr. Whirter had, of course, consented to pose in his own doorway.)

The stranger looked surprised. "The poisoning case? But . . ."

"You must have heard of that," several voices chorused. "The old lady poisoned by her granddaughter . . ."

His face cleared. "Yes. I remember. But was it here?"

"Up at the Hall. They call it the End House. Silly sort of name. Can't any one see it's the end house?"

"And it was here? And Mr. Whirter—where does he come in?"

Mr. Whirter explained with dignity, "The police wanted my reassurances—naturally—that I had not sold morphine to any member of the household."

"Morphine? That is a poison?"

"'Course it's a poison." Daft these foreigners were. Of course in their country it was all knives, flash, stab, and then the body lying untidly on the pavement. Mr. Whirter remembered some lines that seemed appropriate,

> The rug is ruined where you bled;
> It was a dirty way to die.

Took all the romance out of a murder, lines like that. It was quite true what people said, in spite of Ellen's idiotic preferences. Poets could always be trusted to spoil sport.

"Of course it's a poison," he said, his voice indulgent in its contempt. "And you can't get poisons nowadays without a doctor's order. Matter of that I've hardly had a case of morphia in six months. Doctors don't like giving it and that's a fact."

"But you have morphia for emergencies?" the stranger insisted.

"This is a chemist's," explained Mr. Whirter in patient tones.

"Suppose this young lady is not the murderer," suggested the other, in the voice of one who has made a great discovery. "Suppose that some one came creeping into Mr. Whirter's shop when he was, perhaps, out. Suppose that some one to be a clever thief. Could he not—what is your word?—lift the morphia and no one know?"

The idea delighted the crowd. "Well, that's true, isn't it, Mr. Whirter?" said the tobacconist. "I've always thought it a disadvantage not to sleep on the premises. Though I suppose with your family it 'ud be a bit difficult."

"My lodgers are most respectable, both of them," insisted Mr. Whirter, heatedly.

"Oh, but it need not be the lodger," cried Mr. Michael. "Unless, indeed, your lodgers did not like the old lady?"

"Neither of my lodgers have so much as met her. Kept herself to herself she did, and I didn't hear many folk complain. In fact, though remembering the respect that's due to the dead, I must say I've often wondered if Ted Wolfe didn't regret his bargain. He's not half the man he was ten years ago."

"Had his victuals free for ten years," said the tobacconist, aggressively.

"There's more important things than food," said the ironmonger's wife, who had run across the road to find out what was going on.

Mr. Whirter nodded. "That's true. Well, supposing my old ladies—a church worker in the east end of London one of them was for thirty years and her sister a matron in a children's home, according to her own account,—well, suppose they don't want to poison the old lady, perhaps this gentleman," he looked in a steely manner at Mr. Michael, "can tell us who did."

"I do not know the people," protested Mr. Michael, "but there are others in the house, are there not, who might wish to see the old lady in her grave?"

"That's what a lot of us have been saying," said the ironmonger's wife. "Mean to tell me this girl, with all that money coming to her, was going to murder the old lady in a way that 'ud simply be signing her own confession?"

"Ah, but it turns out she wasn't going to have

the money, not if the old lady lived, and she didn't think any one would guess about the morphia."

"Well, if you ask me, there's others I could name a sight more likely to be in it than her. I don't want to make no mischief, goodness knows, but there's a certain gentleman as 'ud find Mrs. Wolfe's money pretty useful to him just now."

"But because a gentleman is married to a wife who is not attractive to him and who is not, perhaps, generous, does he take her life? Are there not compensations for a gentleman in his shoes?"

"That's just what I'm saying," said Mrs. Mead, who was never renowned for discretion, "there are. But they have to be paid for. And they can be precious expensive."

"And has this gentleman never asked Mr. Whirter for morphia?" asked Mr. Michael ingenuously.

Mr. Whirter looked startled. "No," he said in a loud voice. "No one's been asking me for morphia. But I have been asked some pretty queer questions lately." And into his mind there flitted the picture of Ted Wolfe saying, "How many must you take to poison you? Wouldn't half the bottle do it?"

"Would Mr. Whirter know if any one had stolen his poison?" the patient stranger continued.

"Course I should know. I've only got to check up the quantities."

"Then, of course, you know that there is none missing?"

"I could easy find out."

"Always best to keep your poisons in a safe place," said the tobacconist, maliciously.

Mr. Whirter went back to his shop. He examined his poison chest with care. When he came he was smiling.

"No one's been at my poisons. Not a grain of morphine short. No, I didn't think it 'ud be that way."

"There is another chemist here, perhaps?"

"No, there isn't. But what's to prevent a chap going up to London? There's places they say in London where you can get hold of poisons as easy as I could get you a tin of liver salts."

These speculations thrilled and excited the audience. They were so pleased with Mr. Michael for having started this conversation, that several of them agreed to pose for him, on the strict understanding that they weren't liable. Mr. Michael, well enough satisfied with one morning's work, refrained from joining in the general conversation. This dealt, without much pretence at secrecy, with the widower of the Wolfe mystery.

"That was a queer sort of will," some one said.

"Reckon he wasn't too pleased when he heard it."

"I guess old Back was a lot less pleased. There's trouble blowing up in that quarter all right. I'll bet the old man's rare mad about the will. They've always behaved as if they were different flesh and blood from the rest of us. They'll have to crow on another note now. After all, say what you will, a girl in trouble's a disgrace to any man in these parts. 'Tisn't as if it was London."

"Or as if Ted Wolfe could put things right by marrying the girl," said another triumphant voice.

"Not without he loses the money and he won't want to do that, after ten years of having none."

"Happen he thought no one had eyes but himself," giggled Mrs. Mead. "Didn't he know Silas Back was the hardest man in the county?"

"You take care, Ethel," a neighbour warned her. "They can take you to court for saying less than that. I tell you."

"I've said nought," shrilled Mrs. Mead, indignantly. "Nought but what we all know to be gospel truth, if the old lady at the Hall was blind and deaf."

"What's truth got to do with it?" asked some one else, contemptuously. "If a certain gentleman could hear what you was saying, you could be took to prison."

"Happen he'd rather be deaf too for a bit," said Mrs. Mead darkly.

"Happen he would. But, anyway, there's no sense you opening your mouth so wide. You don't want to get yourself mixed up with the police. A nasty nosey lot they are. No respectable woman 'ud care to have them traipsing in and out of her house."

Mrs. Mead had to agree with that. Mr. Michael had heard as much as, at the moment, he needed to know. He finished taking photographs, skilfully elicited names and addresses from his audience, made undecipherable notes against one or two names for his own illumination later, and went back to the Barleycorn. To the landlord, whom he saw in the coffee room where he had his mid-day meal, he said he had secured several commissions and was full of hope.

" All a question of knowing the blarney, I suppose," the landlord said rather ungraciously.

Mr. Michael smiled. " I have been fortunate," he said simply. And then he asked where Mr. Back lived.

" Which Back d'ye want ? "

" Mr. Silas Back."

" He's over at Upfell Farm. It's a mile or more out from here. Know the part ? "

" If you would please explain . . ."

The landlord came and drew diagrams on the tablecloth, with a pepper castor for the farm, and two forks and a spoon for the path the stranger was to take, and a salt box for the chief landmark on the journey. The stranger thanked him politely, and after a brief rest went off in the direction indicated. As he approached the farm he saw the farmer himself, a smart, sturdy figure, with reddish hair and a straggle of red beard. He stopped when he saw Mr. Michael approaching. He wasn't quite sure how to place the visitor. Either an artist or a Bolshevik, and in either case undesirable.

" Looking for some one ? " he demanded in unpleasant tones as Mr. Michael halted.

" You are Mr. Back ? "

" Well ? "

" Mr. Wolfe—of the End House—I have heard of you from him . . ."

" You—did Mr. Wolfe send you here ? "

" He—he——" the mind of the stranger worked quickly. " If I might come in for a minute. It is not so easy to talk here where persons hear us."

" There's nothing to hear us bar the rooks," said

Mr. Back disagreeably. " But you can come in, if you've a mind—if you've got a proper message from Mr. Wolfe, that is. And I'm not surprised," he added fiercely, leading the way into a bricked kitchen, " that he's afraid to write. Might look bad the old lady dying just when he's needing the money so."

" That is what he feels."

" Well, what does he expect me to do ? "

" If you would please say nothing . . ."

" Oh, that's his game, is it ? Did he give you any money ? "

" Not yet," countered Mr. Michael, nervously. " He has not any."

" What about the hundred pounds he was going to bring without fail on the 26th of last month ? Days and days ago. Where's that ? "

" He has not—I do not understand——"

" Stringin' you too, is he ? " Mr. Back was grim with hate. " I'll tell you. He came down here with a cheque—twenty pounds it was—he'd borrowed off one of his wife's relations—on Tuesday night. Keep that, he says, and to-morrow I'll bring you a hundred."

" ' Where'll you get a hundred from ? ' I asked him. And he said, ' I shall have it to-morrow. I promise.' And that's the last I've heard of his blasted hundred pounds."

" Perhaps he does not like—now that his wife is so suddenly dead . . ."

" Well, she's left him plenty of money, hasn't she ? "

" It is not that. But he cannot touch it yet.

Things are difficult, especially with this trial coming on."

"I bet he'll be a lot easier in his mind when the trial's over, and some one else has swung for the murder."

Mr. Michael looked shocked. "But you do not think—you cannot think . . ."

Mr. Back leaned forward. "I tell you, the police might start thinking over again if they knew about this little matter of my girl."

Mr. Michael drew himself up with a jerk. "Mr. Back, sir, you go too far. It is no joke to my friend——"

"And d'you suppose it's a joke to me to have my daughter got in the family way by a fellow who isn't in a position to marry her?"

"But Miss—Miss Back—you all knew he was married."

"We didn't think he was going to play a dirty trick on us, and a girl young enough to be his own daughter, too."

"It is always like that in England," said Mr. Michael sadly. "It is not experience that you value, it is the new thing, the untouched—in Mr. Wolfe's place I would have looked for a plump widow, with a little money of her own, and settled down to a nice smooth home life. But no. He must choose a young girl, unbroken, self-willed, knowing nothing of men; he must make his latter years as restless as these last ten have been. Some men will not learn."

"Well, there wasn't any idea in my mind of my girl getting in this sort of mess. And I want handsome compensation, I tell you. He ought to marry the lass by rights . . ."

"But then, he would have no money," stammered Mr. Michael.

"The old bitch. I might ha' guessed she'd serve him like that. Not that I can't do a lot better for my girl than that. But you tell him from me—it's a thousand pound, or I go to the police with what I know."

"But, suppose you do, what will it gain you? You speak as if you had but to open your mouth, and behold!" he clapped his hands vigorously, "you have already the handcuffs on Mr. Wolfe's wrists."

"Well, and that's pretty well how it would be. I tell you, if ever I saw a man crazy for money, that man was Simon Wolfe. Anyhow, you get back and give him my message. Tell him he's got a week, and then I'll say all I know. And I know the best way to put it, too."

"But, you would not give the young lady away," protested Mr. Michael.

"The young lady's going to give herself away so soon it won't be possible to gloss over things. I see what you mean, though. Ted Wolfe thinks he's going to sneak out of this. Well, he isn't. And you can tell him so from me."

IV

"Now, what was the meaning of that hundred pounds?" reflected Gordon, sitting in the parlour of the Barleycorn, putting together the information he had and trying to build therefrom a coherent pattern. " Had Wolfe really got any money hidden away? And if so, why hadn't he produced it earlier? Why didn't he take it down that night, when things were obviously pretty rough? Instead of that, he got a loan out of Bell, and was so desperate he even tried to get money from his wife. It's pretty obvious that Back was threatening him with exposure, and instant exposure at that. And we can probably take it for granted that Wolfe would be instantly disinherited if that story got to his wife's ears. So between the two of them he was absolutely in despair."

His thoughtful mind moved on another step. " That surely is the explanation of the sleeping-draught. Wolfe was going to get something from his wife's room that night; in view of his promise to Back that can't have been anything except money. I suppose he was on his way there when Blake ran into him, and he had to manufacture the excuse about a drink. Now, supposing he found that money, he'd have taken it down to Back at once. But he didn't. Why not?

" (*a*) Because he couldn't find it.

" (*b*) Because he was afraid of arousing suspicion if he suddenly appeared with money immediately after his wife's death.

" (*c*) Because he'd already parted with it to some one else.

" Now as to (*a*), he'd hardly take such a chance unless he was pretty certain that the money was there. And there doesn't appear to have been anything thrown about or upset, as I'm sure would have been the case if he'd had a frenzied search for it. I wonder who would know anything about it. It might be possible to get something out of Miss John. It follows then that he knew of money hidden in the room, and I think he knew where it was hidden. The point is, was it still there when he went to look for it?

"(*b*) If that's the case, the money must still be in Wolfe's possession. And how am I going to find that out? Bluff, perhaps. If I went up to the house as the emissary of Silas Back I might learn something. Or I might just put him on his guard.

"(*c*) This appears to me improbable. It's only on the stage as a rule that people are blackmailed by two women at once."

It seemed to Gordon that, as he was in the neighbourhood, his next step was to discover whether Wolfe had been able to borrow any money locally, supposing he was foolish enough to try. There was no one whom he could have approached in Aston Merry, but a Mr. Isenbaum lived at Aston Pleasant, and was prepared to lend sums from £20 to £2000. Gordon found the office with a little difficulty, tucked away in a corner of the High Street.

"No," said Mr. Isenbaum, automatically rising to his feet as his visitor entered. He conducted business on quite a modest scale in a bare little office, with no clerk and no one but a nightly charwoman to keep things in order. "No, I do not vant any photographs. If zere is any one who vants to see me and does not know vere I live zat is his loss. Me, I do not need to advertise."

" Perhaps I want to borrow money on the strength of my business," grinned the newcomer. " Perhaps I mean to branch out."

Isenbaum shrugged his shoulders. " A business zat is so small zat it cannot pay its way—and if it was big you would not be coming to me—is no security for a man who has to keep a wife and three children."

" Oh, I didn't suppose you were a philanthropist. Like every one else, you're in business for your health. But suppose I've good security to offer ? "

" And zat is ? " The fat little man's expression hadn't changed ; neither eagerness nor courtesy informed it. It was as blank as a wall.

" I might have a rich wife."

" A wife zo rich zat she will not help you now ? "

" It happens that way sometimes. Women, you may have noticed, are very acquisitive. What they have they like to hold, whether it's husbands or cash. They don't understand the art of sharing." He remembered suddenly he was supposed to talk in slightly imperfect English, and his accent was a little more noticeable as he continued, " Have you ever noticed women in an omnibus ? How they will bargain over pence and count and calculate. Or when they are having tea in a shop. You had a teacake, Isabel. That was fourpence. I had a scone ; that was threepence. They do not halve their bills: And when they are married they do not halve their incomes."

" Perhaps zey are wise," said the moneylender softly, quite unmoved by this rhetoric.

" It is not wise not to help your husband and

not to trust your husband. A man must have money. . . ."

" But not my money," Isenbaum cut in. " I have zeen zo many of zese derelict husbands who want my help, and nozing to offer but hope."

" Oh, yes. That man at Aston Merry, perhaps—but I am not like that. . . ."

" Aston Merry ? What do you know of him ? " Isenbaum's voice was sharp.

The stranger shrugged his shoulders. " I read the papers. I am sorry for him, a man whose wife will not help. What is such a man to do ? He must have money. I was there only a week ago with my photographs. There was a great deal of talk going on. That was natural. And they are saying that he has been trying to borrow money, oh, for a long time. He has been in a difficulty. But it is not like that with me. And I have my work. Soon I shall be a rich man. But I must have a little money now—immediately."

" I zay to you what I zay to all ze ozer husbands who want money and can show me no security—go home, silly man, and make it up wiz your wife and let her help you. She is ze person. . . ."

Mr. Michael seemed to be in no hurry. " It is a strange world," he observed without originality. " If Mr. Wolfe had been more fortunate, if, shall we say, you had been a less good man of business, and had lent him a little money, how different everything might be now ! "

Isenbaum leaned over the counter. " You are crazy," he said scornfully but with some appearance of rage. " I believe you are one of zese missionaries

—dressed up with your camera and your pictures and zinking zat you will make me zay it is my fault zat the poor lady is dead. It is nozing to do wiz me. If I lend money to every man who is in a piece of trouble, I shall soon be worse off than them. Oh," his excitement rose, " so zat is your game? Because I do not lend money to Mr. Wolfe, I—I, mark you—am responsible for his lady's death. Let me warn you," he leaned so far over the counter now that he was doubled in two and his arms splayed out like the fins of a whale, " zat is a very dangerous zing to zay. Every one knows zat missionaries are mad, and no one listens to zem, but all ze zame, you will not be wise to zay a zing like zat in zis place. And Mr. Wolfe did not kill his wife. Ze police have proved zat zat young girl killed her. You are a very foolish man. Zo you may go away, wiz your pictures and your camera and your foolish tales."

Mr. Michael shuffled out of the shop as he had been bidden. He was beginning to feel a bit sorry for Wolfe.

V

While he was in the neighbourhood he decided to go up to the End House, and see if he could learn anything from Wolfe himself. He went still as Felix Michael, still carrying the camera.

To his surprise Wolfe himself opened the door, and said at once, " No, no, we don't want any photographs taken. Don't you know what house this is? " His tone was very jerky and harsh, and the man himself looked slovenly and hag-ridden.

Gordon, with Gallic politeness, intimated that he did not.

"You do, though," said Wolfe, fiercely. "You're like all the rest. Out to make a bit of brass. What's people's feelings to you?" And he added savagely, "I wouldn't ha' come to the door—the blasted bell's ringing all the day—but I thought it might be that slut they're sending up from the village."

"So Margaret Grant's gone, has she?" reflected Gordon, walking back to the inn to settle his bill, before leaving for town. "What does that mean? That our elaborate picture of her relations with Wolfe are just a fairy tale? Or is she just throwing dust in our eyes?" There was, of course, a third possibility, which was that there had been a row, and the pair had separated.

Back in town, he went to see Neville. "There's still a lot to be picked up at that house," he told him, "but I'm not really in a position to do it. I was wondering if you could take a hand?"

"I'd be no good," said Neville immediately. "I'm not on intimate terms with any one there. I only set eyes on Wolfe and Miss John for the first time when I went down for the inquest. I don't see why Anthony shouldn't go. We've agreed he really can't be involved, and he's rather popular with Miss John. She's probably at the conscience-stricken stage now, when she's recalling every harsh word she ever spoke, every pang of impatience or resentment she experienced. Within six months she'll believe her mother was a misunderstood angel. But from our point of view nothing could be better. She'll talk, and that's what we want."

"There's another point," Gordon said. "I'm wondering if Wolfe has been in London lately. We know he didn't get any morphia at Aston. John might find that out, too. Mrs. Wolfe's collapse must have fixed things pretty well in Miss John's memory. Besides, he may have tried to get money."

CHAPTER III

I

ANTHONY found his Aunt Dorothy in deep mourning, with jet round her throat, and large jet buckles on her flat-heeled shoes, in her own room, reading Emerson on Happiness. She jumped up in a very flustered state when he was announced, and thrust the book back into its place on the shelf.

"Oh Anthony dear. This is delightful. But if only you'd told me you were coming. Probably nothing nice for lunch. It seems so heartless to enjoy one's meals with dear Car only having skilly, isn't it? Or is that just the comic song? But anyway I'm sure it isn't nicely served, and I always say service makes such a lot of difference. I'd rather have a sandwich on a linen cloth with fresh flowers than the best dinner in the world served anyhow without so much as a paper rose in the middle of the table. And speaking of roses, aren't you looking pale? Of course, it must be dreadful for you. You've always been like brothers and sisters together. And Derek, too. Have they let you see her yet?"

"I haven't seen her. But Neville's been down pretty often. He swears he'll get it all right or chuck his job. He knows Car didn't do it."

"Of course, dear, so do we. As if any of us would let ourselves think anything else. I admit imagination is sometimes difficult to rein in, but when it comes to letting ourselves believe anything like that of Carol—well, what's the use of discipline if we can't just ignore unpleasant implications? Is Mr. Neville a clever man, dear?"

"He's supposed to be pretty bright. He's Norman's friend, originally, but we've all known him sometime. We got him, because he used to flutter a bit round Car. Thought it might weigh down the balance."

"Oh, I'm sure if I were a man I should flutter round her too. Such a sweet-looking girl and such a good housekeeper. Not that lots of men don't prefer them dark, of course," she added hastily, remembering Rose, "but somehow she is so very attractive. And her cakes—so light, Mama used to say, plenty of women can do all the nursing I need, but how many of them can cook?"

"Grandmother was a good business woman," agreed Anthony cordially. "You don't mind my coming, Aunt Dorothy? By the way, where's Wolfe?"

"I hardly ever see him now. We have meals together, because the servants complain if we don't. But, really, he seems quite stricken by mamma's death. As if he feels he hadn't appreciated her enough. Of course, one always does feel guilty after a funeral, and then all that food. It seems so heartless to eat when they're lying underground and can't have a bite, especially when they did enjoy good food so when alive. But dear me, how I ramble on. Yes, Wolfe. I try and tempt him. But no, it's not a bit of use. Perhaps he's worried over Carol. And of course it isn't nice to have your wife poisoned. People will talk so. And perhaps it wasn't a very wise marriage for either of them. But you can't see these things ahead, can you? And they say marriages are made in Heaven, and we are told no cross, no crown, but I never liked to say that to Mama, and I'm afraid Wolfe isn't a very religious man. At least, he wouldn't come in to tea when the vicar called. Such a comforting man, Anthony. He wanted to know *everything*."

"I'll bet he did," said Anthony. "Are you going to stay on here indefinitely? And Wolfe?"

"Well, no, I don't think I should care to do that. I thought of coming up to London."

"What on earth would you do in London?" asked Anthony in amazement.

"There's always something going on in London. And the Parks. And I shall enjoy seeing shops again. There really is so little choice in Aston Merry and if they send for things they never seem to fit. And, of course, later on I shall be giving up my black, because I always feel it's so wrong to mourn."

"And then I should so much like to live in one of those nice London hotels, somewhere in South Kensington, say. Not being accustomed to house-keeping, and servants being such a trial. I used to know a very sweet woman who stayed at what they called a private hotel. So convenient for the omnibuses, she said."

" Well, I will say this for the place, supposing you don't mind boarding-houses and incense, you can nearly always find a taxi cruising about, which is more than you can say of most London districts. Just for emergencies, you know."

" Well, dear, I don't suppose I shall have many of those," said Dorothy resolutely, rather as if emergencies were fleas.

" Ah ! " contributed Anthony, who seldom had anything else. " When do you think of going ? "

" Oh quite soon. I couldn't stay here now."

" It's Wolfe's house, isn't it ? "

" I suppose it is, but I'm sure he won't want to stay here. He'll go back to a farm, I expect."

" By himself ? "

" Oh, he'll have to have a housekeeper or something. Or he might adopt a child. It'll be so lonely for him. You do need some one as you get older. I'm sure I was often thankful I hadn't married, because Mama would have been so lonely."

" Wolfe might marry," suggested Anthony.

" Oh no, dear, not now. Not when it would mean his losing all that money."

" It's going to be dull for him, isn't it ? "

" I daresay he won't be any duller than he was here. After all, he must have friends."

" Well, I suppose that means the place will be sold. What does Wolfe do with himself all day ? What did he do when grandmother was alive ? Did he never go up to London or have a holiday ? "

" Not very often, dear. She liked to have him here. Well, it was natural."

" Oh quite," agreed Anthony. " Why buy a nice

dog for some one else to walk out? It 'ud be quixotic to the point of absurdity to think of the dog's feelings."

"I do wish you wouldn't talk like that, dear. It does sound heartless, even if you don't mean it like that. And then I don't think Wolfe knew many people in London. I remember the only time in months that he did go mamma wasn't at all pleased. I've sometimes wondered if getting so upset about that—she was accustomed to having her own way, you see—didn't help to bring on her last attack."

"Just before she was ill, was it?"

"Yes. He'd been talking of it for some days, but when mamma really was ill, I thought he wouldn't go, of course. But he did. The very day dear Carol came down. I suppose he thought mamma would be all right in her hands. Such a capable girl, and so dreadful to think that all that energy may be lost. Still," she looked flustered, grabbed at her subject and went on hurriedly, "I was afraid she might think it rather rude, but I don't think she minded."

Anthony said gently, "Aunt Dorothy, are you sure about the date?"

"Well, really, dear boy, I think . . ." Dorothy opened the drawer of her dressing-board; this was largely concealed by a sofa and the skilful disposition of cupboards and mirrors. She took out a book with a black shiny cover, and began to look rapidly through it.

"I always like to keep a diary," she confided in warm excited tones. "It's good practice, for one thing, and then when you come to write letters you can look through and find something to say. A letter that only covers two sides of a sheet looks skimpy, ungenerous, don't you think so? I like to cover three sides anyhow. Of course, one feels its rather waste to leave the fourth, but then the recipient can always use the blank sheet for notes or shopping orders. That's what I always do. I keep a little box for slips of paper, and then I'm never at a loss. Ah, here we are. It was the 21st. That was a Friday."

"It was. We dined with Derek on a Thursday. By the way, is there any truth in the rumour that's flying about that Margaret's deserted you already?"

"Oh yes, very sudden. I did hope she would stay while I was here. But she said she couldn't afford to take any risks."

"Risks of what?" demanded Anthony, genuinely intrigued.

"It seems she had the chance of buying a little business, a shop of some sort, in Bruton—North-East London, I think that is. A little paper and sweet shop, and packets of tea."

"I know the kind of thing. What made her choose that?"

"She said she didn't wish to be beholden all her days, whatever that may mean."

"Oh, just that she wants to establish her independence. Well, she'll probably make it pay. She's the right kind. Where did you say the place was?"

"In Bruton High Street, just opposite the church, she says, though I shouldn't have thought that helped much, unless she's going to stay open on

Sundays. Nobody's going to church on week-days. The old couple who had it have been trying to sell for some time, so she got it rather cheap."

"I bet she would," remarked Anthony, grimly. "Has she always been a capitalist?"

"She seems to have plenty of money, because she said she'd forego her wages in lieu of notice if I liked. Of course I gave them to her, though I know Mama wouldn't. She said she'd been looking forward to this sort of thing for ages, but hadn't had the money."

"And now she's drawing on the legacy? Can she, till the trial's over?"

"No, dear, it seems she can't. I was talking to that nice Mr. Nicholls about it. He came to know how I was off for money, and told me to draw on him, if I were short. He said I couldn't claim a penny till everything was settled, and the country—that was the queer way he put it—had decided who really did kill Mama."

"So Margaret has come into money lately?" thought Anthony. "Now where would that come from, unless our suspicions are right and she's been blackmailing Wolfe? Poor devil! If he had the whole lot of them at his throat. It's a pity we don't know more about that couple. I wonder how I could find out."

Then, in pursuance of his plan, he began to talk of himself. "Changing addresses seems to be in the air. I'm moving, too. My landlady wants too much rent, and when I suggested she might share some of her profits with me and reduce her terms, she told me haughtily that even the poor had to live, precisely the point I was trying to make myself. As a matter of fact, I suspect her of being an extremely rich woman. One of these days you'll see paragraphs in the evening papers, headed Recluse's Secret Store. 'When the police broke down the door of a dingy one-roomed flat in Houns-ditch this morning, they found the emaciated body of Mrs. Agnes Lamb, dead, on a straw pallet. Search revealed large sums of money in gold and notes behind the mildewed wallpaper.' She's the sort of woman who wouldn't trust banks."

"Mama was a little like that," Dorothy confided. "I don't mean she didn't trust them exactly, but she said there was always some risk, and as she didn't intend to be buried by the parish she kept enough money by her to pay for her funeral. But I think she must have meant it as a joke, for when she died we only found two pounds and some silver in her purse, and no money in her room at all."

"However economically you do it, you'd hardly manage a funeral for that," Anthony agreed. "But perhaps she hid it in a hidey-hole you haven't discovered."

"She always said it was in the bureau in her room," said Dorothy, doubtfully. "But I suppose she must have taken it out some time."

"When, like the rest of us, she was short of cash. I wonder how much it was."

"I'm afraid I couldn't tell you, dear. I've never had to arrange a funeral, so I don't know what they cost."

Anthony let the conversation pass to other topics.

He had learnt what he wanted for the moment. When he went his aunt said, wistfully, " It has been so nice seeing you, dear. You must often drop in when we're both living in London." It suddenly struck him as horribly pathetic that she should so hunger after life in a second-rate boarding-house. It showed you what existence must have been like for her up till now.

II

" I think," he reflected, walking back to the station, " this answers (*a*). The money was there and Wolfe got it. Grandmother wasn't the kind that says one thing and means another. (*b*) He didn't take it down to Back because he'd already parted with it. Which brings us to (*c*) and the answer is Margaret Grant or I'm a Dutchman."

He was meeting Neville and Gordon in the former's room on his return, and to them he detailed the history of the day's activities.

" I wonder, supposing all this is correct that we're imagining, that Wolfe didn't split up the money and keep them both quiet for a little. He had more coming soon. I suppose it was £100 that was hidden there. Well, fifty on account is something to be getting on with."

" That's a good point," Gordon agreed at once. " It seems to me there's only one answer to that. He didn't, because he couldn't."

" You mean a single note ? " exclaimed Neville. " It ought to be possible to trace it, if that's the case. It should be fairly easy to trace Margaret

Grant down. We know roughly where she is, and in a neighbourhood like that you can always pick up a lot of gossip about newcomers. We want to get in touch with the people who sold the business, and who might, presumably, have the note."

Gordon said, "I'll go to Bruton in the morning. Meanwhile, there's work to be done this end. We know Wolfe needed money, and since he couldn't get it locally he may have tried the London money-lenders. There are plenty who advertise loans on note of hand only, and Wolfe, living as he did, and not being much in the way of brains at the best of times, would probably go to them. We could circularise them. They'd remember him all right, whether there'd been a deal or not, since presumably his only security is his dubious position as part-heir to his wife."

"We know he didn't raise anything," said Anthony. "If he had, grandmother wouldn't be under the sod now."

"That's slander and libel," Neville warned him grimly. "Well, Gordon, you get on with that, will you? And let us know what happens."

They were still discussing details when the telephone rang and Neville, removing the receiver, began one of those maddening one-sided conversations that enrage the rest of the company.

"Yes. . . . It is. . . . No. . . . I am. . . . Yes, do. . . . At once? . . . Five minutes. . . . I'll detain them. . . . Right."

"That was Norman," he told them, replacing the receiver. "He says he's got something to tell us about morphia, though he doesn't know it has any bearing on the case. But we can't afford to be particular. Everything must be fish that comes into our net. He's coming round at once by taxi."

Norman arrived in little more than the stipulated five minutes. He grinned at Anthony, and said, "I might guess you'd be on the spot. I tried to get Derek, but he was out. I thought his novelist's imagination might be useful to us. I've warned Rupert already that I don't suppose this will be a scrap of use to him, but your brains may work faster than mine, and see hope in it."

He took a chair and a cigarette and began his story.

CHAPTER IV

He had said farewell to one patient and had a welcome half-hour's respite before he expected the next, when his secretary-receptionist came in and said, "There's a lady, a Mrs. Phillimore, would like to see you, Dr. Bell. No, no appointment, but she seems very anxious. She says you attended her when you were staying at Deal two years ago."

"When I was at Deal?" Norman reflected. Certainly he had taken a golfing holiday at Deal two years ago, and had stayed at an expensive and famous hotel. And quite likely he had seen this Mrs. Phillimore. He generally found that it leaked out you were a doctor and ten to one some one called on you and you couldn't refuse, however disinclined you might be for a busman's holiday. Personally he never blamed the clergy for taking their vacations in turn-down collars and red ties. Some one or other was at the poor devil for a death-bed or a sick-bed or a troubled conscience half the time, if he was once recognised in his true colours.

Norman frowned. "What's she like?"

"Middle-aged, rather excitable. The kind that wears a dozen bracelets and shakes them all at you."

"She sounds just the sort of person who would be at Deal and want attention," agreed Norman mournfully, "but why me, I wonder? Another of these hysterical cases of personal magnetism, I suppose." He had had experiences of the kind before. Probably this woman had taken a fancy to his appearance or his voice or some inexplicable quality he himself wouldn't recognise as his, and had made up her mind that she would be cured by him or no one. Norman didn't want to see her; he liked his patients to have doctors' recommendations, but on the other hand he had a singular reluctance to send any one packing without a word. You never knew what Providence might not deposit on your doorstep, and when he said that he wasn't thinking of a fortune or a title. He really did care for the technical side of his work.

Mrs. Phillimore rushed in, all her bracelets clanking, her glasses slightly crooked, her mouth thickly and unevenly rouged, her brown eyes snapping behind their powerful lenses, a bead bag swinging perilously from one wrist, her boa trimmings flopping on an artificially produced bosom. She carried a novel and a bag of odorous bananas.

"Oh, Dr. Bell—or should I say Mr. Bell?—I am so sorry not to have made an appointment. I really should, but I'm such a creature of impulse. And then I thought the fates might be kind again, as they were that year at Deal."

Norman put her into a chair and picked up a silver pencil. "I'm sorry. I'm afraid I don't remember. Perhaps you'll tell me about yourself."

"Oh, but I mustn't take up all your afternoon. I'm sure you're busy too. And not even an appointment. Besides, I'm in rather a hurry myself. There's a sale on at Horne and Betters and I always think you get such good class things there. And the people so civil. I cannot endure shops where the assistants are not polite. I'm sure it's not to please myself, I always tell them, that I shop there. And I'm quite ready to take my money elsewhere if I can't be treated with civility. And since you're in too much of a hurry to serve me, I'd like to see the manager. After all, it's what they're paid for, isn't it?"

"Oh, quite," said Norman, noting automatically some of her typical peculiarities. "Now if you'll tell me your trouble, Mrs. Phillimore. By the way, what is the name of your doctor?"

"I—oh, I don't live in London, you know, and my doctor died only the other day. I wonder if you could recommend me one. I'm at Portland-le-Hope. Such a dear little village. Quite out of the world. Man has forgotten it for a generation, and now they're running a bus from the Tottenham Court Road twice daily and three times on Saturdays. It seems somehow to despoil the peace. As I say, there's only a new young man there, and I wonder if you could tell me anything about him."

Norman said quite firmly that he couldn't. "If you could remind me of the circumstances in which we met," he suggested.

"Oh yes," agreed Mrs. Phillimore glibly and with relish. "Of course. They're as clear in my mind as if they all happened yesterday. I'd had a nervous breakdown. Voices, you know. From beyond the grave. Specially my husband. A very difficult man, Dr. Bell—you did say it was Dr., didn't you? Always so sure of himself and so unsure of me. Giving me advice. As if I'd ever taken it when he was alive. And what proof have I got that he knows any more now? He never could learn anything. And so misleading even to-day. Telling me horses that are going to win races and never do, making me lose my money. Telling me about shares and so on—things I don't understand any more than he does. And perpetually fussing. He was always a fusser, was Malcolm. If I was making a cake in a round tin he'd come and stand by me and eat raisins and say, Why don't you make it square? When we had a baby girl he said, Why didn't you have a boy? So ungrateful. And serve him right when Providence took the dear little baby back again, though the fuss he made then. . . . That kind of a man, you see, doctor. It isn't as if I wasn't a good wife to him; never in seventeen years did he put on unaired combinations, and I'd go round with him to make sure he'd locked up properly. Kept down his expenses for spirits and found out which of his friends really weren't doing him any good, and got rid of them for him. No use wasting your money on men who simply want you to buy their drinks. And as if he didn't plague me enough then, he's neglecting his new job to plague me now. Just like Malcolm. He couldn't stick to things. Says he misses me so much. Well, what I say is, he ought to have his hands full now, and it's a pity if all those spirits aloft can't keep him in order. Why, I was only a wife, and *I* wouldn't have let him go interrupting a widow's sleep of nights. Especially knowing how I need my eight hours. And now he's begun again. I've lost nineteen pounds in horse racing this week; I thought perhaps at the end of two years he might have learnt something. But not Malcolm. He could hang about at 10 Downing Street and not come back with a single bit of news you wouldn't find in yesterday's paper. Well, the only thing for me to do is to get a good night's sleep and let him maunder on by himself; and the only thing that makes me sleep is that tonic you gave me; and I want you to give me another prescription, if you will."

Norman looked puzzled. "If you had written to the chemist . . ." he began, but she shook her head. "Oh no. You'd have to give me another order."

Comprehension began to impress itself upon her companion. His manner was instantly steely. "I don't quite understand," he observed inaccurately.

"It had morphia in it," said Mrs. Phillimore, "and the chemist warned me that if I wanted another bottle you'd have to give me another prescription. That's why I came myself. I didn't think it would be any use writing—you mightn't remember me——"

Norman pressed a bell under his desk and the secretary-receptionist came in. He made a movement with his hand and Mrs. Phillimore cried out, "What does this mean?"

"I think you'd be wiser to go without any fuss," Norman advised her coldly. "It's a criminal matter to attempt to get morphine by false pretences."

"Of course, I didn't get a penny out of it," he added, "though she'd taken up twenty minutes of my time, which is expensive. That wouldn't occur to her. She's the kind that wastes an hour of a shop-assistant's time, and stares if you remonstrate. That's what they're there for, she'll say. I shouldn't have come dashing round here to tell you all this, if it weren't that it gave me an idea. Suppose whoever did poison grandmother got hold of the morphia in just this way? There's a lot of that sort of thing going on. Listen and I'll tell you the rest of the story."

Mrs. Phillimore, he said, had not been gone long before a second unexpected visitor put in an appearance. Norman had been expecting a serious case of arrested shell-shock, in which he detected signs of incipient mania. It had caused him a good deal of anxiety, and when he saw the stranger's card:

MR. JOSEPH WYLIE

and heard from his secretary that the gentleman was connected with the police, he began to wonder anxiously if his patient had suddenly become much worse and run amok, doing serious damage.

"I hope to Heaven it isn't that fellow," he thought, really startled now. He turned with outward composure and inward trepidation to meet the newcomer. A tall man with noticeably square shoulders, wearing a blue suit, with rather thick brown hair inclined to wave, and a brown moustache, came in. He wore a pair of thick nappa gloves, and had left a bowler hat outside.

"Sorry to disturb you when you're busy," he said in a bluff voice, "but this is a serious matter, and we feel you may be able to help us."

"Yes?" said Norman interrogatively, offering a chair with reluctance. He felt this was the sort of fellow who might keep you half the evening.

"Yes. We've got several men out on the watch, and we've pulled in some of the culprits. But there's still a leakage. Now, doctor," he leaned forward impressively, "you have a lot of dealings with nerve-wrecked people, men and women, people who're ruined by drugs in some cases?"

"Yes," acknowledged Norman cautiously.

"I suppose they never let out where they obtain their drugs?"

"It's not of much concern to me where they come from. I have to deal with the consequences." After all, there was professional etiquette; he couldn't give away confidences to the first bobby in a reach-me-down suit who asked for them.

"Do they ever ask you to prescribe drugs for 'em?"

"They're not lunatics, as a rule," said Norman dryly. "And they wouldn't be coming to me if all they wanted was to continue the habit."

"Well, our information is that there are people

going about, particularly women, trying to coax drugs out of doctors by all kinds of tricks. They pretend they've had prescriptions before—what's that? Oh, so they have been at you?"

Norman had started. The coincidence seemed uncanny.

"As a matter of fact, only this afternoon a woman I'd never seen before tried that game on me. One gets accustomed to various sorts of bluff, certainly, but it so happens that I haven't been approached in that way hitherto."

"Did she give you a name?"

"Mrs. Phillimore."

"And an address?"

"No. I didn't ask her for one. When I realised what she was up to I had her shown out."

"Did you tell her it was a criminal affair?"

"I warned her."

"I dare say she's gone all down the street pitching the same yarn. What did she look like?"

"Dark, rather primly dressed, sort of district-visitor look about her. Wore gold earrings, very talkative. . . ."

The visitor chuckled. "So she's calling herself Phillimore now, is she?" He wrote it down in a little notebook. "Alias Bella Pratt, alias Lady Joan Snow, alias Miss Margery MacIntosh, alias Madame Ferrier . . . oh, her list of pseudonyms is as long as a modern literary critic's. What was her game this afternoon?"

"Oh, voices—nervous trouble. I thought at first it was a hoax till she asked for the medicine I'd made up for her two years ago at Deal."

"With some sort of drug in it, I suppose?"

"Morphine."

Mr. Wylie nodded. "Yes. And other times it's been cocaine. These women are mad, they'll take any chance. But they take a lot of trouble. She had to find out you were at Deal two years ago. They're as crafty as eels."

"That's my only experience," said Norman.

"You haven't had strangers admitted when you've been out? People who say they'll take a chance of getting an appointment when you return? That's another trick of theirs."

"Would that help them? They couldn't help themselves to my drugs in my absence. They're all under lock and key."

"Lock and key? You don't suppose that's going to deter them, do you? As a rule they give themselves plenty of time, telephone in some one else's name to find out when you're expected back and then turn up. There are enough men and women going about in society to-day who can open any ordinary lock, yes, and even a complicated one, neatly enough, to make a formidable thieves' kitchen. Another trick of theirs is to pretend to be a relative who's expected. That doesn't always come off, though I've known cases where it was very successful. I wonder if you could ask your receptionist if she has let any one in during your absence, particularly some one who has decided he can't wait for your return."

Miss Phipps was called in. She said, "D'you mean just lately?" and Norman said, "I check my store of drugs every month, about the 10th, so it's nearly due again. They were all right on the 10th October. Can you remember any one suspicious coming without an appointment since then?"

Miss Phipps looked up her diary; she had a large book in which she noted the names of all visitors, very fully annotated. Norman described her as one of those girls with an itch to write, but no creative or original ideas. She said that on the 21st, at about five-fifteen, a man came asking for Dr. Bell, saying he was a cousin passing through London, who very much wanted to see him. The secretary told him that Norman was out, and the man said he'd wait. His train didn't go till a late hour of the evening, and he knew no one in London. Miss Phipps settled him in the waiting-room with a paper, warning him that Norman might not be back till half-past seven. At six o'clock she left; the stranger was still there.

"You know what the big houses in Cavendish Street are like," Norman went on. "Enormous basements so far down that it's practically impossible to hear footsteps overheard. That man had the whole run of the ground floor to himself. He could have gone into any of the rooms, done what he pleased. Of course, he shouldn't have been left alone, but Miss Phipps never doubted his story. About half-past six my man went upstairs, and was surprised to find no sign of the visitor. He looked round suspiciously, but nothing appeared to be missing, so he came to the conclusion that the chap had to catch a train, and had just oiled out. I came back about eight o'clock to go to the —— Hall with Derek to hear this new violinist, who, by the way, justifies everything Hayden told me about him; he plays like a angel—so I didn't wait for a word. I'd barely time to snatch a sandwich and go out again. When Miss Phipps told me about it in the morning I thought it was a cousin on my father's side, who descends upon me every now and again, usually when he wants money. So I rather congratulated myself on missing him. I haven't written to him since, and he hadn't written to me. However, when Mr. Wylie became so serious about this leakage of drugs, I sent a pre-paid wire, asking if he'd been in town on the 21st. The answer came—well, you can see it for yourself." He tossed the slip of paper over to them. It read

"No such luck. Broke to the wide."

and bore no signature.

"Is it pure coincidence," asked Anthony slowly, "that Wolfe was in town on the 21st?"

CHAPTER V

I

It was too late to do anything that night, but early the next morning Gordon went to a Typewriting Office and arranged for circulars to be sent to practically every moneylender in London. It had been agreed that Wolfe's name and particular circumstances should not be mentioned. It would be enough to say that the writer was trying to trace a man corresponding to Wolfe's description who was missing from his home, and was believed to be suffering from loss of memory. He was known to be penniless, and it was thought he might have tried to raise money in London.

"Because none of these fellows will want to be mixed up in a criminal case, if they can help it," said Gordon with the wisdom of experience.

Having given these instructions, and arranged for an address at a small hotel near Charing Cross, where all communications should be sent, he went to Bruton and began his inquiries for Margaret Grant. It was not difficult to track down the shop; and a woman standing in a doorway at the farther end of the street supplied him with plenty of local gossip.

"Not been there above a week," she confided to the bewildered looking man who asked directions. She supposed him to be the agent of one of the many philanthropic societies that work among the poor—verifying references, perhaps. Unless the newcomer was trying to get a bit of help to get the business going. Though the woman hadn't been there above a week, already there were changes. She had put a counter down one side of the shop—quite a big shop it was really, though Mr. and Mrs. Morris had been portly, both of them, and had seemed to fill it up a lot. But this new woman hadn't any flesh to waste; she was serving tea and sandwiches, and doing well. She was the kind that 'ud make money anyhow, and no one but herself to spend it on. Funny, the way life was.

Gordon asked why the old couple had given it up,

and was told they'd always wanted to retire to the sea before they died. They'd gone to Leigh now, a nice street about five minutes off the front, up a bit of a hill. Ever such a nice house called Hillcrest, though it was only half-way up really. Gordon strolled past the new shop, seeing evidences of old-fashioned customs being ruthlessly dusted out of sight, while efficiency ruled at the till. There were several customers, and the shop looked clean and attractive.

" I'll be coming in one of these days," he thought, " but to-day I'll just buy a paper, in case that woman at the end of the road's watching me, and then I must go down to Leigh."

II

The sedate elderly couple he had come to visit had been at their new home no more than a week; to them the bright staring little villa with its pocket-handkerchief of lawn in front and its patch of vegetable garden behind represented bliss. It is not many people who attain an ideal, but Mr. and Mrs. Morris were among the number when they saw their red plush overmantel triumphantly erect on the dining-wall, their bamboo whatnot with the lacquer brackets and curly trimmings in the pink drawing-room, their handsome blue enamel double-bed, with painted roses—hand-painted, mark you—on the panels, in the top floor front, their nice rose-patterned toilet set on the light walnut commode, their decorated drainpipe for umbrellas in the diminutive hall, and their nice brown velour cloth on the dining-room table, in the brand new little house with company's water, electric light, a kitchen ten feet by five, matchwood walls and a showy porch with a light hung in it, not more than a quarter of an hour from the sea. For twenty-seven years they had been making two ends meet in the little confectionery and tobacconist shop in Bruton, one of the outlying districts of North London. It had often been hard work for times of late had been cruel hard, but the coming of electric hares had helped, because men wanted the paper about the dogs, and it was fashionable to give children more sweets in a week than Mrs. Morris had had in a month when she was a little girl; and tobacco—you could generally count on that. Still, it had been hard work, and sometimes the little house at Leigh had dipped right over the horizon and Mrs. Morris had believed she would die in the dark hot little room at the back, with its diminutive window and smoking fireplace the landlord wouldn't do anything about. She'd shed a lot of tears in that room in her time, had Mrs. Morris. But now the new woman who'd bought the place could cry there, if she'd a mind, though she didn't look to Mrs. Morris the sort of woman who'd waste time crying anywhere. Time would be her slave, not she his, which was probably right. Anyway, she was handsome in a hard sort of way; and if any one could make a shop go she'd do it. You got to know the type. Hadn't given them as much as the place was worth, either, but Mrs. Morris had had a sudden fit of terror, as though, if they refused this chance, they mightn't get another till it was too late, and all her joys now seemed fixed on the unassuming longing to die within sight of the sea.

So they sold the little business, goodwill, stock and all, for cash down, and they were out within four days. Mr. Morris had had his eye on one of these little houses for some time; they'd been down here August Bank Holiday and gone over the model one, and whispered and nudged and hungered. And it still seemed like a dream to get up in the morning and look out at the little garden and hear the sea —as Mrs. Morris declared she could—and know they belonged to themselves at last, and not to the shop. She had already ceased to wonder how that woman was getting on.

Mrs. Morris was dusting the incredibly-decorative dining-room, with a blue cap over her nice grey hair, when the stranger came to the door. He was a tall young man, dark, neatly dressed. She thought he probably wanted her to take out an insurance—represented some daily paper. Even at Leigh you weren't free from that kind of thing. But though she appeared, brisk and ready to say No, thank you, though politely, because even in an age of rush she hadn't forgotten her manners, it turned out that the young man hadn't come from a paper at all. She was rather vague as to where he had come from, and she called her husband.

" Here, father." (Though all the child they'd had had died at six months old, and never any more hopes.) " A gentleman about the shop."

Mr. Morris, a short, square little man, blue-eyed, limping slightly because these sea-winds touched up his sciatica, came forward.

" You'd best see the lady that's got it," he said resolutely.

" I'll be seeing her later," promised the visitor. " Now, there's nothing for you to get worried about, but the fact is there's a little confusion about the money she paid for it."

" The money . . . ? "

" Yes. I wonder if you'd mind telling me if she gave you a cheque or ready money, or what ? "

" Here, what's all this about ? " demanded Mr. Morris.

Mrs. Morris asked more quietly, " Do you mean, mister, there's some talk of the money being stolen ? "

" Certainly not. The fact is there are a number of forged notes in circulation, and there's some notion that this lady—Miss Grant, isn't it ?—may have paid for this business with one that was, of course, passed to her quite inadvertently. Of course, if she gave you a cheque . . ."

" She didn't," said Mrs. Morris, white-lipped. " She gave us a note for a hundred pounds—I'd never seen one before—and she wrote her name on it, because what were we to do with a note that size ? "

" And you paid it into the bank or the post-office ? "

" No. We didn't. We keep our money by us. Then you know it's safe."

" Do you mean to say we're to lose that money ? " Mr. Morris's sturdy resolution wasn't proof against such a possibility.

The stranger was quick to reassure him. " Oh,

no. If we find that this note is one of those for which we're looking, you'll be recouped in full. I can assure you of that. In fact, I've money on me now"—he pulled out a bulging wallet. "It's important to get that note to headquarters. We're making inquiries. So if you've got it handy . . ."

The old lady went off, and Mr. Morris made a series of disjointed remarks about the weather and the situation generally, until suddenly he said, "How's the lady getting on with the shop, do you know?"

"Very well, I believe. She's started a line in sandwiches. Always a fresh ham in cut, and a loaf under the counter."

"Going to make a kind of Woolworth's out of it before she's through, I can see," observed the old man with displeasure. "What was good enough for me and mother won't do for her seemingly."

The stranger said nothing, and a moment later Mrs. Morris reappeared carrying a note for a hundred pounds. The stranger examined this carefully, held it up to the light, pored over it with a magnifying glass, and finally said, "Yes. One of them without a doubt. And Miss Grant wrote her name on the back. I'll have to take this along with me for the inquiry. But I'll give you ten ten-pound notes in its stead. . . ."

"Well, really, I shan't be sorry to see that go," Mrs. Morris agreed. "It don't seem right to me to have nothing to show for all that money but a bit of paper. These now . . ." She collected the ten-pound notes lovingly.

III

In the little shop at Bruton, Margaret Grant was carefully weighing out two ounces of ham, cut thin. Her customer, a small sharp-eyed woman, glued her eyes to the scales. They didn't quite tip down, and Margaret cut off a shaving, chiefly fat, to redress the balance.

"You'll be one of these rich ones one of these days," said the customer sarcastically. "Wouldn't give away any of the breadcrumbs even."

"Fourpence," said Margaret calmly. "What's yours, sir?"

She took the coppers warm from being held in a woollen-gloved hand, and turned to a tall, dark, neatly-dressed man who had entered during the altercation about the ham.

"I wonder if I could have a word with you," he said quietly. "Perhaps we could go inside." He nodded towards the room behind the shop.

"And perhaps all the children in South Street 'ud like to come in and help themselves while we're talking," agreed Margaret grimly. "If it's honest, you can say it here."

"It won't be me that minds," observed the stranger gently. "It's about this," and like a conjurer producing a rabbit from a tall hat, he laid the hundred-pound note on the counter.

Margaret Grant was startled, but not discomposed. "What about it?"

"I was wondering if you could tell me where you got it from?"

"And who are you that I should tell you that?"

" You could come down to the station and tell 'em there, if you liked; but it wouldn't really look well, when you've only just come here, to be seen going down to the station with a plain-clothes man. But just as you like, of course."

" It was my money," said Margaret, fixing her dark eyes on her companion.

" No one suggests it wasn't. I only wanted to know if you could tell me where it came from."

" The post office, I suppose. I had to draw some savings to buy this place."

" No, not the post office. The post office have been looking for this note for some time. This and some more like it."

Her eyes were hard, shrewd, implacable. " That's nought to do with me."

" Probably it isn't. But it's necessary for us to know where that money came from."

" I suppose Mr. Morris is complaining?"

" He'd no idea, till he was told, that it was a note for which any search was being made. Perhaps, if you were to consider, Miss Grant, you could tell us where you got it from."

Margaret Grant looked obstinate. " I don't see how you can expect me to remember that."

" It oughtn't to be very difficult. After all, your employers would hardly pay you with a hundred-pound note. And if you'd had it any length of time you'd have put it into your savings account and it would have been traced long ago; so you must have had it recently. And you can surely remember the names of the people who, during the last few weeks, have given you a note for that amount."

"I don't see that it's any one's affair but my own."

"We're not making a criminal affair of it. The point is, that if you got it recently, whoever gave it to you has probably got the other notes in the same sequence that we're anxious to trace. Now, you paid this over as soon as you left Aston Merry, didn't you? So the odds are it was given you by some one there, in token of your faithful service, perhaps. And why not?"

She turned her sombre, unhumorous gaze full upon him. "Why not? It's clear you didn't know that household if you can ask that. Why not, indeed? Because, if you didn't coax it out of them with a gun or a hatchet, you'd be lucky to get your wages and a scrap of sugar for your breakfast-tea."

"And yet some one gives you a hundred pounds. We know it wasn't Miss John, and none of the old lady's grandchildren will own to giving it you; and the old lady herself didn't surely? So it must be Mr. Wolfe."

"Seems like it," agreed the other, without emotion.

"Mr. Wolfe? A kind of pourboire for twelve years' service in the house?"

"I'd earned something. You don't save much on the wages they paid you."

"But of course there was the annuity. Mr. Wolfe knew about that."

"Happen he did, what of it?"

"Only that it seems odd he should have given you a hundred pounds in addition."

"I was able to do the chap a service, and he was

grateful, which was more than most of the people in that house was."

"It was a pretty big service, wasn't it?"

"That's his affair and mine."

The stranger opened his mouth to expostulate, when a young woman with a shawl over her head came in for a bit of ham, and a little boy rushed in demanding a pennorth of mixed surprises, coloured cachous in a transparent orange envelope, a balloon, a brown paper elephant and a pink wooden whistle.

Her visitor had time to collect his thoughts while Margaret Grant satisfied her customers, and when she turned back to him he asked, "Was it before the old lady's death that Mr. Wolfe gave you the money?"

"That's right."

"But you didn't pay it into your account."

"I knew I'd be buying a business one of these days, pretty soon now. . . ."

"So you'd made up your mind to that before Mrs. Wolfe died."

"I didn't mean to end my days going up and down other folk's stairs."

"But surely you didn't intend to leave Mrs. Wolfe's service during her lifetime? You'd automatically forfeit your annuity if you did."

"Well." Margaret shrugged her shoulders. "I knew her kind. Keep you there forty years on a promise, and after she was dead you'd find she'd changed her mind at the last."

"And you were prepared to sacrifice your chance for a bare hundred pounds?"

" Mr. Wolfe didn't give me the hundred pounds to get out, if that's what you mean."

" Then why ? You mustn't treat me like a sucking-child, you know. A man in Mr. Wolfe's position doesn't give you a sum like that for nothing."

" I never said it was for nothing."

" No. Then, Miss Grant," he leaned over the counter in a menacing manner, " I suggest that Mrs. Wolfe had actually given you notice, which of course involved the loss of your annuity, before Mr. Wolfe gave you this money. Well ? "

His voice changed ; now it was light, steely, inflexible.

" Mrs. Wolfe never gave me notice. She never had cause."

" Then why did Mr. Wolfe give you this note ? Did he feel he owed it you for something, some favour, perhaps, you'd done for him ? "

" You keep your dirty thoughts to yourself," cried Margaret. " I've never had any man near me, and never want to neither, seeing the way they serve women."

" Then why did he give it you ? "

" Well, if you must know, I knew a thing or two about him he wouldn't want his missus to know, and he thought he'd square me. Mind you, I never asked him for a penny."

" He just came and thrust the money dumbly into your hand."

" He said, Here's summat for you, or something like that."

" What was it you knew about him ? "

" Oh, well, nothing much."

" Something worth a hundred pounds."

" I never put no price on it."

" Perhaps it was something you'd seen ? "

" Happen it was."

" Something you saw the night Mrs. Wolfe was poisoned ? Eh ? " He laid an accusing finger on her powerful wrist.

" What are you trying to tell me ? I was in my bed that night. I never saw anything."

" Sure ? "

" Of course I'm sure."

" You didn't, for instance, see any one—Mr. Wolfe or any one else—come out of Miss Carol's room ? "

" Are you trying to mix me up with the murder ? "

" I didn't say so. Mr. Wolfe didn't ask you to put a little powder or anything in Mrs. Wolfe's invalid food that night, tell you it was a sleeping-draught ? "

" He did not. And I wouldn't ha' done it anyhow. I wouldn't want to be mixed up in a poisoning."

" Oh, then you don't think it's absolutely impossible that he might have wanted to poison his wife ? "

" If all the men that 'ud like to poison their wives went on to doing it, you'd want a new cemetery for females only," returned Margaret grimly, and without any sign of humour.

" He'd never threatened her that you know ? "

" He wouldn't be such a fool as to do a thing like that with me standing by."

" True. He'd have too much sense. Still, every one knows they weren't a compatible couple."

" I don't know what that means rightly," said Margaret with some dignity, " but if it's anything to do with having separate rooms, then I think, considering her age and everything, to say nothing of switches all round the mirror, she was quite right. That was one of the decent things she did do."

" But a bit hard on him ? " suggested the officer.

" Dogs return to their vomit," retorted Margaret astonishingly.

Her companion wasn't quite sure what to make of that. " He wasn't altogether inconsolable, you mean ? "

" He wasn't gentry, and it was natural to him to go back to what he was accustomed to."

" As he did. And that was what you knew, and he paid you a hundred pounds to forget ? "

" What's forgotten's forgotten," Margaret insisted.

" Not in the police courts, though, not unless you want to do three months."

" What for ? "

" Contempt of court. I see. He, of course, was terrified of the old lady disinheriting him if she got to know about his philandering. . . . How did you know, by the way ? "

" The old gentleman, this girl's father, that is, and me was by way of courting once, and though I broke it off long ago, he still used to talk to me sometimes."

" And didn't he expect to go halves in the hundred pounds ? "

" Oh, there's no end to what a man'll expect."

" But perhaps he didn't know you'd got it."

" P'r'aps you think I'm like a church lady going

round with stomach mixture in one pocket and tracts in the other, giving 'em away with both hands ? I've had to work for my living."

"And when did Mr. Wolfe give you that money ? It would be an awful pity," he added meditatively, "if you were to tell me one story and he told another. Susannah and the Elders over again, you know."

"What's that ? And who was she ?"

"The first recorded detective story," said the officer. "It comes from the Bible."

"Oh, one of them indecent stories ! And then they talk about giving the Bible to the young. I'd as soon give 'em a packet of dynamite."

"Well, and coming back to my question. When did he give it you ? Before Mrs. Wolfe's death or after ?"

Margaret visibly hesitated. "He gave it me before."

"I wonder where he got it from. He was admittedly almost without a penny. He couldn't even give money to his young lady. Miss Grant, are you quite certain . . . ?"

"Well, as a matter of fact, I woke the morning that Mrs. Wolfe died and there was the money in an envelope shoved under my door. And that's the truth, so help me God."

"I see. Well, Miss Grant, it may be necessary for us to ask you to repeat some of that evidence in court. I don't say it will, but it may be. In the meantime perhaps you'd like to make a statement embodying what you've told me."

"What, write it all out ?"

" Yes. Unless you'd rather come to the station and dictate it there. The sergeant'll take it down."

" I'm not going to leave my shop and p'r'aps lose custom. I'll write it out myself and you can take it with you. You'll have to wait a bit, though. Here's some customers."

She served a young man with a packet of Woodbines, a little girl with a penn'orth of liquorice mixture, a little boy with a gob-stick, an elderly woman with a packet of twopenny biscuits, a young woman with her confinement close upon her with some peppermint bulls-eyes and two ounces of tea. Then she turned back to her visitor.

" What do you want me to say ? "

" Just that you received this note—copy the number—from Mr. Wolfe in payment for your silence. . . ."

" They can't take me up for that, can they ? I'd as much right to sell that as I have to sell tea."

" He'd have to bring a case against you, and he won't be anxious to get into any more trouble. Oh, and put it about the time you got the money."

He watched her write out her brief statement and sign it. Then he took it from her. " Thank you. Oh, and don't worry about the counterfeit note. We're convinced you were innocent in that regard."

CHAPTER VI

I

WITH the statement in his pocket Gordon turned towards the railway station. He had ascertained that there was a train to Aston Pleasant, whence he could journey to Aston Merry by omnibus, at 4.39. The journey took nearly an hour, and it was a twenty minutes' run from there, so that it was practically six o'clock when he reached the End House. He asked for Wolfe. The new servant demanded his name.

"It wouldn't convey anything to him, but perhaps you would tell him it's an officer in connection with the inquiry into Mrs. Wolfe's death."

The most obvious quality about Wolfe, when he appeared, was fear, absolute stark terror. The big man seemed somehow to have fallen to pieces during the past month; his firm solid cheeks were loose and their high colour diminished; he experienced difficulty in disposing of his arms and legs; he started at a sudden change of tone. If he had poisoned his wife, his surface advantages were imperceptible; probably the fates had merely dealt him a dirty blow when they let him marry Bertha John.

"Oh, Mr. Wolfe, I'm making inquiries about some bank notes that have suddenly turned up, after they have been the subject of a lot of speculation and inquiry for a considerable time. There are several of them, part of a larger number that were forged, very brilliantly and almost flawlessly, some years ago. The majority of them were traced, but some we have never been able to locate. And then quite suddenly one was presented at a local bank a week ago. I have it here." He produced it.

"Oh, yes?" said Wolfe, in colourless tones.

"This was passed by Miss Margaret Grant, who

was until recently, in service here, to Mr. Morris, from whom she purchased a little general shop at Bruton. He could identify it easily enough, as he had never had a note for this sum before, and he asked her to write her name on the back, which she did, as you will see. There's no question about that being a forgery, as I have seen Miss Grant, and she admits to doing so. I asked her to explain where she got the note from, in the hope of tracing the others, and she told me that it came from you."

"From me? Why on earth should I be giving her notes of that value?"

"She told me that too. And one quite appreciates your motive. It would have been more than unfortunate if Mrs. Wolfe had got wind of this—er—association. And in the circumstances perhaps a hundred pounds was not an excessive sum. I'm not here to question your action, but I am anxious to know whether you have any of the other missing notes?"

"Er—no. I haven't."

"I see. Then perhaps you can tell me where this one came from?"

"I—I chanced to have it."

"But where did you get it from? Who passed it to you? It's very strange, if it has been in circulation, that it has not come into our hands before, when we have been looking out for it sedulously."

"I've had it for some time, to tell you the truth."

"Some years, you mean. . . ."

"Well, I wouldn't go so far as that."

"It's some years since we started hunting for

these. If I may ask, what was your object in keeping it hidden ? "

" Well, a kind of nest-egg, you know."

" For an emergency ? "

" Yes."

" And the emergency arose when Miss Grant tackled you with her knowledge ? "

" Well, yes."

" And yet, when Mr. Back was insistent on compensation for what he, in his old-fashioned way, called the wrong you had done his daughter, you were compelled to borrow money to quiet him ? "

Wolfe was scarlet and shaking. " I—I don't understand. . . ."

" Mr. Bell," Gordon told him pitilessly. " And you'd hardly dried the ink on the cheque before you were down to Mr. Back with that, begging him to keep his mouth shut. And promising him £100 the next day without fail. Queer, isn't it ? "

" What's the matter with the note ? " asked Wolfe, abruptly turning the subject.

" I told you, it's forged. Of course, we can trace it, a note of that size. But it would have made things easier if you had been able to tell us where you got it from."

" As a matter of fact, my wife gave it me a long time ago."

" And you kept it all that time ? "

" Yes. It's a bad feeling to have no money by you."

" But did you ever expect to encounter a worse emergency than the one you were in already ? "

" I—don't know what you mean ? "

"Why, that Miss Grant was at you for money, and Mr. Back wanted money, and I dare say Miss Back wanted money. It seems queer that you didn't do something to pacify them while you were trying to raise more."

"More?"

"Yes. Oh, we know you've been trying to raise money on your interest in your wife's will. And we know it was unsuccessful. But having this hundred pounds laid by, it seems queer you shouldn't have used that first." He leaned forward. "Believe me, Mr. Wolfe, it'll be much better for you if you make a clean breast of things now. Where did you get that note from? And why did you spill the sleeping-draught on the tray of the invalid food? To mislead people or because you were nervous and didn't notice? It's a pretty bad fix you've got yourself into, and your only hope now is to be candid. If you aren't, well, surely you can see the conclusions people will draw. And I must say I don't blame 'em."

Wolfe suddenly collapsed; his knees actually gave way under him and he staggered against the table. "All right," he said in a hollow tone. "I'll tell you the truth. God knows what you'll make of it." And this is the story he told.

He admitted the affair with Winnie Back. She was a pretty girl, and he was sick of his monkish life with its persistent overseeing up at the Hall; the affair had been going on for more than a year, and all would have been well but for the fact that Winnie suddenly discovered she was going to have a child. She had been terrified, had asked Wolfe to take her away, or, alternatively, since he assured her that that was out of the question, to arrange for her to go somewhere where she could have her baby without any publicity. After it was born, of course, Wolfe would have to help to support it, though the young mother was prepared to do any work she could get. But unquestionably it was a responsibility. It hadn't gone through the mind of either to try to evade this charge, once they realised their position. But Wolfe had been desperate. He knew that it meant a lot of expense if the girl went away from home, and he didn't know where he could turn for money. He had nothing of any value, and the few pounds he managed to get out of his wife would be useless to meet the emergency. He had besought Winnie to be patient, and has assured her that he would somehow meet his obligations, but he hadn't known how he was going to keep that promise. Winnie had asked him again to take her away, but that was out of the question. As he said, he had endured Bertha for ten years and he didn't see why he should lose his reward now, when by all accounts he hadn't got much longer to wait. Winnie had said she was terrified of her father learning the truth—he had already promised her a leathering if he caught her carrying on with a married man—and Wolfe was at his wits' end to where to turn. He had tried to borrow money but had found his security too shaky. He had withdrawn every penny from his secret post office account long ago; he had in desperation borrowed twenty pounds from Norman, with no possibility of paying it back. Then he had resolved on a desperate coup. He knew his wife kept a hundred pounds in notes in a locked cupboard in her room. She had often spoken of them; he knew exactly where they were kept. If he could lay hands on that hundred pounds he thought he could save himself. He didn't look into the future; it might be months before his wife discovered her loss; he didn't see why she should ever trace it to himself. Of course, if she did, she would cut him out of her will at once, but if she learned the truth about Winnie Back, she would do that anyhow. On the Wednesday he had learned that she wasn't going to die after all, as every one had expected, and he was desperate. He got Norman to give him the prescription for a sleeping-draught. He had wanted veronal or chloral or something that would ensure her being unconscious when he broke into the room; afterwards he had regretted the question, since it had done him no good and might merely arouse suspicion. However, he made the best of an unsatisfactory position and went down to Whirter's where he got some sleeping tablets. He asked a number of questions, because he didn't want to poison his wife, but on the other hand he didn't want any chance of her waking while he was in the room. He had crushed the tablets, as the coroner suggested, and tipped the powder into the invalid food as soon as Margaret, who put it on the little table in the passage, had gone downstairs again. At about midnight he had determined to take his chance and look for the money, and on his way he had encountered Derek. He had hastily pretended he wanted a drink, and to his annoyance Derek offered to come with him. He had gone down and poured himself out a stiff one and had come stealthily upstairs again to find the corridor deserted. He knew that his wife never slept with a locked door, and if any one did disturb him he was resolved to say that he had had premonitions and had come to see if she was all right. But he counted on not being found out. He had entered the room without any trouble, and had stood quaking on the threshold. After an instant he said in low, clear tones, " Bertha, did you call? Did you call? I heard a voice," and then approaching the bed switched on the bedside lamp. No one passing would distinguish that light, as it was heavily shaded. His wife had been fast asleep, and switching off the lamp he made for the cupboard. He knew where his wife kept her keys and he had not even had to force the lock, though he had been prepared to do this. He found a single note for a hundred pounds at the back of the drawer. This he removed hastily and relocked the drawer. Then, he said, he had had the most extraordinary sensation of fear. He was not an imaginative man, and he was, as he said, cold sober, but as if a finger of terror had touched him, he found himself unable to move. At first he felt as though he were in a supernatural presence; and then he was convinced his wife was sitting up in the bed behind him, watching him with gleaming, ironical eyes. He had been so desperately afraid that he hadn't dared turn round. At last he said her name several times, adding, " You've got me all right. But it's your own damned fault. Why could you never treat me like a human being, let me have enough money in my pocket? You can't take it to the grave with you." Still there was no reply from behind him, and with a quick jerk he had swung himself round. The room was shadowy, ghostly, and he couldn't detect any upright figure in the bed. He crossed the room clumsily, feeling that now it didn't matter how much noise he made, and switched on the bedroom light. His wife was lying in exactly the same position as when he entered, but there was something about her face that alarmed him; she scarcely seemed to be breathing, though, he said, a very faint movement of her breast convinced him that she was alive. But he thought—this is the end. It's the end. What a fool! I needn't have taken the risk. Suppose I'm seen coming out of the room? It even passed through his mind to return the money, but at that thought his fear took another shape. He saw them all ranged in front of him, Margaret, Old Back, Winnie, all demanding and threatening, and clutching the note in his hand he slipped out of the room. He was still fully dressed. The comb, he thought, must have slid out of his pocket as he bent over his wife. He admitted he had put his hand practically to her breast to try to detect signs of breathing. He had put the note into an envelope and slipped it under Margaret's door. The first news that greeted him in the morning was that his wife was dead; at first he thought only that he needn't have taken that chance, and then that he had known this last night. And, following on that, came the frightful shock that she had been murdered. At once he had seen the weakness of his own position; he had even wondered whether he had misunderstood the chemist and had himself administered a fatal dose; but the news about morphia had reassured him on that point. He hadn't, of course, dared to tell the truth when he was questioned, and Margaret had kept silence also in a policy of self-defence. She probably thought him guilty, but he swore this was not true; he didn't know whether Carol had really done it, but said that when she was in one of her moods Bertha almost drove a man out of his mind, so that for the time being he was scarcely sane, and he thought she might have this effect on the long-suffering Carol.

"Well, I can't discuss that, and anyway it isn't my job," said the officer. "It's *sub judice*. But if you take my advice you'll tell the truth at the trial. You're bound to be called as a witness. You're much more likely to get off if you do than if you stick to your original story."

Then he asked him to sign a statement, and Wolfe asked if he'd write it out and he, Wolfe, would add his signature. This took almost an hour, and then Wolfe said nervously, "You—what about a bite? You must be pretty peckish." But the officer said he must get back to London; he'd get some food on the train.

II

Gordon had installed a man in the room in the Charing Cross Hotel, in case of an early answer to the letters, that would catch the midday post. As he came into the room his aide-de-camp, a man called Taylor, said cheerfully, "You're just in time

There's a chentleman called Graham on his way here now." And a few minutes later a page brought up a dark, clean-shaved man, with high cheekbones and a long bony nose.

"Sit down," Gordon offered. "It's good of you to come round. You may have realised it's a matter of some importance."

Mr. Graham said quietly, "Yes. Where there is a woman's life at stake matters are bound to be important."

Gordon's brows went up, but he only said, "You will appreciate that I could hardly be absolutely candid in a circular."

Mr. Graham bowed. "Of course not. But the photograph was a good one."

"He didn't come disguised, then? No, he wouldn't. Would you tell us what happened?"

"He said he wished to raise money immediately for a temporary embarrassment. He could offer us no satisfactory security; he was dependent, it appeared, upon his wife, a lady a great deal older than himself and in poor health. He said that he expected to come into the greater part of her fortune. He did not think she would be likely to live more than a year or two. All this was satisfactory enough from our point of view; we frequently lend sums, sometimes quite large sums, to gentlemen with expectations, but when we carried the conversation a step further it appeared that the gentleman could offer no proof of what he said. He could not refer us to a solicitor; there was nothing to prevent the lady from changing her will, he could not even name a figure that he expected to inherit. He was, in fact, in the position of the dependent husband who cannot wring any funds out of his wife, and is not even sure what his position will be when she dies."

" Did he take your refusal hard ? I imagine there was no transaction."

" There was no transaction. If I may say so, his appearance was that of a man utterly at the end of his tether. I think he had had unsuccessful interviews with other firms during the day. It must have been close on six when he left us, having argued for nearly an hour, but of course without success. We should be ruined if we did business on those terms. As he was going, he asked if there was a public house near. The lad who showed him off the premises said there was one at the corner, and watched him go in. I hardly think he would have had time to see any one else that day."

When Graham had gone Gordon said in disappointed tones, " I didn't realise how much I was counting on Dr. Bell's story. I believe I really thought the mysterious stranger was going to be Wolfe, but Graham's knocked that on the head all right. So we're back at the beginning again, and nothing proved, after all."

CHAPTER VII

I

GORDON spent a restless twenty-four hours examining every scrap of evidence against Wolfe, testing every shred of speculation that had been offered in his disfavour. But turn and twist it how he would he did not find anything that linked Wolfe with the murder. Unquestionably he had drugged his wife, and then robbed her ; but Gordon became increasingly convinced that of the murder itself he was innocent. It was, therefore, necessary to find another suspect. Gordon collected all the evidence, all the papers he had on the case, notes he had made, letters he had received, and went through them with a tooth-comb. Whenever he discovered a fact that told against a particular individual he noted it on a slip of paper. He spent a whole day in this manner, taking into account the psychological differences of the various members of the household, as well as their motives and opportunities to commit the crime. Patiently, like a cracksman negotiating a stubborn safe, he went over and over the various points at issue, until suddenly the solution broke upon him, a solution so shocking that even he, hardened as he was, could scarcely accept it. When, however, he compared it with the facts he possessed, he saw that it fitted at every turn. Motive, opportunity, previous knowledge—none was missing.

He was still brooding over the position, wondering alternately how he could have been so blind, and how on earth he was going to break the truth to Neville, when the lawyer was announced.

" I've been chasing a concealed will in the next street," Neville told him, " and I thought I might as well come in and see how our case is going." He frowned. " I wish to goodness we could get something decisive. Derek's going all to pieces. He rang me up a couple of hours ago like a cat on hot bricks. He's been to see Carol again and he says she's beginning to collapse under the strain. I told him we were straining every nerve. Anything new turned up ?"

Gordon said slowly, "I'm not surprised about Blake. It must be a terrible time for him."

"With his girl in prison ? Precisely."

"I didn't mean that exactly," Gordon admitted. "I mean—knowing how hard we're working to get Miss John out of prison—and terrified that we may succeed."

II

Neville did not make the violent protestations Gordon had expected. After the initial shock was passed, he said, "Explain, will you ? Have you stumbled on something fresh ?"

"No," Gordon acknowledged. "I wonder I didn't see it before. I suppose we were so hot on Wolfe's trail, and on the face of it Blake seemed such an unlikely murderer that we didn't pay much attention to him. But you remember at the beginning we discussed the possibility of his being the culprit, and there was quite a strong case against him."

"We agreed he'd hardly be guilty because he was going to marry grandmother's heiress."

"Yes. When she was her heiress. That might have been twenty years ahead. Apart from that, he had what he earned, and we know how far that went in paying his bills. We know he had creditors descending in every direction ; he was even threatened with the possibility of being turned out of his rooms. And he is not, as his cousin, Anthony, is, a man who can cut his coat according to his cloth. Blake has a conviction that certain things are necessary to him, and therefore he must have them. Poverty and discomfort he can't face. And he needs security, too. That's why, when he had dropped the morphia into the invalid food as he came downstairs that night, he later, when his cousin was with her grandmother, substituted water for the morphia. It was a frightful risk—that he might lose the forty thousand, but it would be better than losing his life. And he hoped the trick would never be discovered. I know what you'll say, what they'll all say. That Blake was in love with his cousin. But how did he show it ? It didn't prevent his getting into debt ; it didn't make him work harder or try and save for a home. He just meant to live on her money. I know all this cant about art not stepping down from her pedestal, but its net result is that artists expect to be kept by the State without any of the attendant disadvantages." He paused and drew a long breath. " Do you remember his saying that he'd overheard his grandmother remark to Marshall that they shouldn't marry on her forty thousand pounds ? You don't hear whole phrases like that if you're running downstairs. You only hear if you stop outside the door for some purpose ; and the invalid food was outside the door by that time. Then consider. He knew what his chances were going to be. He'd heard of the summons ; that meant he would be on the premises himself within two or three days. If his grandmother died this time, he was all right. If she didn't he was absolutely ruined. So she's got to die. He knew she was having morphia; he's admitted it. It wouldn't be difficult to see she had an overdose. The only trouble was getting hold of the stuff."

"Then you think he was the man in Norman Bell's house on the 21st?"

"Who else? It couldn't have been Wolfe, because the only time that any one could have got at Bell's stores was the afternoon of the 21st and the only person who called at the house came between five and six, and stayed half an hour, and just after five Wolfe was with Mr. Graham, and just before six he was waiting on the steps of a public house for the doors to open. That quite clears him. And doesn't Blake fit in with all the facts?

"Hadn't Bell made him a present of the fact that he was going to be out all the afternoon? Hadn't he been on the premises when the S.O.S. came the previous night, and seen Bell take the morphia? He's resourceful and imaginative; he needed both those qualities to plan the crime. And he planned it very well."

"All this is circumstantial," Neville objected.

"More men are hanged on circumstantial evidence than any other kind," retorted Gordon swiftly. "It's often the only kind available. Of course, we aren't near the end of our case. We shall have to get proof. But I think this time we have got our man."

" He couldn't have known he would have the chance of substituting water for the morphia."

" No. That was a surprise to him, another gift of chance. That's why I said he was resourceful."

Neville was silent for a long time. Stealing a sideways glance at him, Gordon thought he wouldn't care to be in Derek's shoes when the pair met. The man looked absolutely murderous. But, after that endless pause, he only said, in a queer dragging voice, " Norman will be less surprised than any one. Less shocked, too, perhaps. They say you can't shock a doctor. He told me that Carol was sick with fright when she discovered Mrs. Wolfe was dead. Norman was convinced she thought Derek had a hand in it. I pooh-poohed it, of course. I know she trembled and was pale, but then it was a bitter morning, and she was under the open window while Marshall was examining her. God knows how she'll take the truth."

III

There was no doubt at all as to the way Rose was going to take it. She was violent, contemptuous and incredulous in turns.

" Has Rupert gone out of his mind ? " she demanded fiercely of Anthony. " Or doesn't he really know Derek in the least ? Oh, I don't mean he mightn't commit a murder. Any of us might, if it comes to that. But not this sort of murder. And not with the blame falling on Car. Why, he was going to marry her. He'd have married her if she hadn't had a penny. He cares for her. It's nothing to me that the evidence seems to be against him, thought personally it doesn't seem to me so much evidence as just a stringing together of some stray facts into a pattern that pleases you. But—I care a good deal for Derek myself; I always have, and I know—I know he couldn't do a thing like that."

"I don't think that's frightfully logical," Anthony objected.

"Never mind about logic. What about Derek? What can we do? Get another lawyer?"

"If Derek's found guilty he can employ one. I don't see that we can do much in that direction."

"Derek won't let it get as far as that, whatever he may say. If there's really going to be all that stink, he'll get out."

"Go abroad? Oh, but he can't. He's not under arrest, but he's been unofficially suspect as Car's accomplice ever since the inquest. He won't be allowed to go about like a perectly free person."

"I didn't mean go abroad. How insufferably dull you are to-day, Anthony. He'll take the only alternative way out, and he shan't do it, Tony, I swear he shan't. He's innocent, even if nobody at present knows that but him and me. There must be some one. . . . You can't really believe he did it."

"It's a pretty rotten sort of thing to believe," Anthony confessed. "He's one of us, you see. And one's own people don't do that kind of thing and then slink out like an alley cat. Which," he added dryly, lighting yet another cigarette from the stub of the last, "is an attitude of mind that's about as logical as yours."

"Well, it's no use our asking one another till Kingdom Come who it could have been. We want to get it thrashed out by some one fresh. What about the Home Secretary?"

"That's after the trial," Anthony reminded her gently, "if you want a reprieve."

"Is there no one else? Doesn't Parliament provide any one?"

Anthony clapped his hands so suddenly that Rose swore at him. "I wish you wouldn't do things like that. Can't you realise that this matters more than my life to me?"

"It was your saying Parliament that upset my balance. Do you realise who grandmother's member was?"

"No; they're all too much alike, and whichever party's in power the same things seem to get done or not done."

"This chap's an exception. His name's Egerton. You must have heard of him. He used to represent a Yorkshire constituency but last election they brought him down south. He solves murders in between doing his political chores, as other men do crosswords. He was in the Penny case, you know, the Hanging Woman of Menzies Street, and that old French actress they found stabbed, and—oh, several others."

"And would he be any use to us?"

"If he'll take it on. We can't force him."

"I could force a stone," said Rose grimly.

"His reputation is that he never refuses anything a constituent puts to him. And grandmother certainly was that."

" She's dead, of course, . . . It's a pity we aren't accusing Wolfe."

" Well, the murder took place in his territory."

" Yes. Let's try him, anyhow. He can but refuse."

IV

Walking up the long cool passage in the House of Commons, Anthony was struck by a sense of the secret history even at this moment being made in those great halls and shut-off rooms, whose doors they passed. He was touched at once by a sense of the past; on these very stones where his steps now softly rang, other men in different garb but of like blood, burning with similar hopes, with dreams and visions akin to his own, had passed to their varying fates. His spirit was hushed immediately to a sense of proportion, almost of insignificance, as if the one or two tiny people they represented in this tremendous pageant of blood and courage, of ambition and achievement and fear, really didn't loom so large against the vast background as during the past weeks it had seemed they must.

Rose thought of nothing but Derek.

They hesitated for a moment, while they filled in the official card, as to the reason they should give for their demands on a man who wasn't even their own member.

" If it's personal, put personal," the policeman at the barrier advised them kindly. " No need to go into details on a card."

" Will he come for that ? " asked Rose in her

shrewd way. "Won't he feel he's seen enough people who want to lure him on to talk of themselves?"

The policeman smiled tolerantly. "You don't know Mr. Egerton, Miss. It's my belief he'd see a stray kitten if it could write its name."

Anthony laughed unwillingly, and put Personal. He really wanted to put Aston Merry Murder, but thought Egerton might be ruffled and therefore less willing to help them, if he did so.

They had to wait a long time; there was an international debate in progress, and though neither was a politician each knew that a man like Egerton wouldn't stir till the salient points had been disposed of. Other men seemed less conscientious. Every now and again a Member appeared, his appearance being heralded by a stentorian roar from one of the policemen.

"Mr. Jones. Mr. Jones."

And sometimes a figure would detach itself from the little group gathered round the rope barrier and approach the newcomer. The members took their visitors away to stray corridors, where they sat on green or red velvet cushions under enormous historical paintings. Anthony noticed that the majority suffered no sense of discomfiture at the gravity of their surroundings, but plunged each into his little trouble as if that marked the horizon of his world. Several people turned and looked at the distinguished young couple standing a little apart from the crowd. They were worth a second glance. Anthony tall, elegant, debonair, his fine clothes outlining his slender figure, Rose *soignée*, composed, all there, said one man to himself, turning to throw an extra glance over his shoulder, with her red beret pulled firmly over one eye and a red felt flower in her perfectly-fitting dark coat. You couldn't teach either of them anything about the value of clothes.

Close by, a large man, rather like Mr. Pecksniff, thought Anthony (who could be distracted anywhere off the stage), was interviewing a timid girl in a fawn-coloured coat and the wrong kind of hat. She was applying for a job as secretary and he was asking innumerable questions.

"There's bound to be an election pretty soon," he boomed at her. "Now have you done electioneering?"

"No. But I've done a little political work."

"For a member?"

"For one of his agents." She mentioned a name. Pecksniff screwed up his face.

"And now tell me something about yourself. Who's your father?"

The pale girl said eagerly that he was a stockbroker, she mentioned his firm . . .

"What cheek!" exclaimed Rose impulsively. "I wouldn't be asked all those questions if I wanted a job. He isn't engaging her father. And she won't get the job either. No girl who's such a fool as to let herself be bullied like that will get any job anywhere."

Then at last a voice behind them began to call with powerful monotony, "Mr. Egerton. Mr. Egerton."

V

Egerton was tired, he looked, to-day, more than his five-and-thirty years. It had been a difficult afternoon, and he hadn't carried his amendment. You couldn't make the House as a whole realise the gravity of the position; a third of them didn't even trouble to attend the debate, and of those who did, a number slipped away before voting time. The world, as Egerton saw it, was in a nasty mess, and the few people who cared about it were groping like ants in a vast Babylon surrounded by ruins that might collapse on their heads at any moment. He had particular troubles, too, in his own constituency; unemployment was rife, and men who had suffered damage in the war, and recovered from it, were slipping back into their ancient disabilities; the spirit of dogged hope was breaking, and in its place came fear, dereliction, defiance; it might eventually break into open rebellion. Egerton, who deplored all unscientific and unconstitutional methods, had to admit that he couldn't blame the participants if it did.

Then he looked up and saw his visitors, and immediately he knew a stab of fresh hope. He was like that, capable of deep feeling for all his imperturbability; people complained that you never saw him tumbled or at a loss, as you did ordinary human beings; that smooth, fair hair seemed to remain smooth even in a blizzard, and nothing marred the perfection of his tailoring or his carriage. But when he saw those two, young, reliant, fearless, with something sturdy and undefeatable about them, he forgot the appalling conditions for a moment, thinking, "If our age can produce that kind of fineness and beauty, there's hope and to spare yet."

Anthony did most of the talking. Egerton had recognised him already; he seemed to mix in all worlds and to participate in all interests, and a face or a figure that interested him remained in his memory for ever. He wondered if the girl were Tony's wife. Anthony disillusioned him. "You've read about the Aston Merry poison affair, I suppose," he suggested. "We're mixed up in that."

"Of course," said Egerton, placing them both at once, "I have just read the general position. I haven't studied it."

"Mrs. Wolfe was your constituent, and her husband, of course, still is."

"Quite. But he's in no danger, is he?"

"No. I'm only explaining really why we've come down on you, seeing we both live in London."

"I don't quite see what you want of me," Egerton confessed.

"We want you to spot the flaw," broke in Rose.

Egerton looked a little taken aback. "I suppose you aren't often asked to lend a hand in murder cases," Rose continued. "So far they've just been your friends, haven't they?"

Egerton smiled, and Anthony chuckled. "I'm not often asked to take it on as part of my parliamentary work," the former admitted.

"We wouldn't ask you if we weren't at our wits'

end. Though, really, it's not as odd as it might sound. The House of Commons makes laws and upholds justice, and all we want is to make sure that justice is done. And at present it's going very badly off the rails."

"I take it you represent Miss Carol John's defence?"

"No. Derek Blake's defence. We've been trying to find who really did kill grandmother, as obviously it wasn't the kind of thing Carol would do; and all the evidence we've got together points to Derek Blake. And, of course, he's just as impossible as Car. I mean, he's one of us; he wouldn't do a thing like that."

"And you want me to pursue inquiries?" Egerton was courteous but perplexed.

"Oh no. I don't think anybody could pursue them further than we've done. Greyhounds after electric hares aren't in it with us. Our trouble is that we've mixed the ingredients wrong, and so we haven't got the right answer. What we hope you'll do is to go through all the papers and the evidence and the letters we've got, and see where we've gone wrong."

"If any one can find out, sir, we feel it will be you," Anthony broke in deferentially. "I realise, even if my cousin doesn't, that this is right outside your province, but when you're desperate you'll break all the rules of the game, and I agree that Derek Blake can't really be guilty. It would be too foul."

"And if I read all these papers and agree that he is the culprit?"

Egerton's clear intent gaze flickered from one to the other.

" You won't," said Rose simply.

" If you think so, sir, we shall know it's right, however incredible it seems. But I, like Rose, feel it can't come out like that."

" And it's rather urgent," Rose broke in. " Derek, you see, knows the position. And if we aren't quick, rather than have all this publicity about him and Car, he'll put an end to things."

" He won't do that till he's utterly desperate," remarked Anthony coolly. " Derek's like me, he knows life's worth a lot and he's got heaps of work he wants to get done. He won't chuck it until he's forced to."

Egerton, who could no more have turned his back on such a request in such circumstances than a magnet could refuse to attract a needle, gravely took the bulky case of papers they had brought with them, and promised to go through it within forty-eight hours.

" I think everything's there," said Rose.

Egerton looked rueful, and Anthony grinned. " We wanted to make it as clear as possible, so you wouldn't be hung up by gaps and uncertainties," he said quickly. " It's a hell of a nuisance when you've no one on tap to question and find you're blocked through lack of information."

" Oh, I appreciate your forethought," said Egerton politely. " Where can I reach you ? "

" I've put the address and telephone number of all of us, and Rupert Neville, our solicitor, on a card inside. You might want to question any one of us. And we'll all be at home to-night and to-morrow night. It is, as my cousin says, pretty urgent."

"Well, I never saw such a bandbox Bertie," observed Rose clearly, as they left the building. "It only shows that you can never tell what's underneath. Even you, Tony, under your beautiful clothes, that I'm sure you haven't paid for, may be a mine of unsuspected violence. There's my bus. Ring me up if you hear anything." And like a flash, radiant and vivid, she was gone.

CHAPTER VIII

I

It was midnight before Egerton had a chance of examining the bulky packet he had been handed in the House of Commons. He was going out to a dinner he couldn't scratch and, when he returned, there was a letter by the last post that necessitated a good deal of telephoning and inquiries, and finally a prepaid telegram. But at last Rosemary betook herself to bed, and Egerton went into his study, switched on the small desk light and sat down to his task. Rupert had thoughtfully given him a family tree,[1] so that he shouldn't confuse the various cousins, and had made a full note of the contents of the will and the general financial position of every character in the play. So that

[1] See Frontispiece.

Egerton started with a clear picture of the general situation in his mind. He put out a hand to turn the lamp so that the beam fell obliquely across his bent fair head, and on to the hands that should have belonged to a surgeon and seeemed wasted on a mere M.P. (one, moreover, who didn't even dabble in art as a hobby), and on the flawless set of the coat. Long ago his friends had told Egerton he'd never be driven to Guardians' relief whatever the state of the country; any of the big ready-to-wear firms advertising in the underground would be happy to give him a job as a living advertisement at any time.

It was six o'clock when Egerton put the papers down; every now and then he had stopped and muttered some comment; once or twice he had made notes on a jotting pad at his elbow. At six o'clock he rose stiffly and pulled back the curtains. To him it was clear enough who had committed the murder, though proving it was going to be another matter. It meant letting other things slide, probably for several days. He went slowly upstairs and turned on a bath, thinking what a comfort constant hot water was. A man's voice said out of the shadows, "Can I get you some tea, sir?" and he looked up to see his man, Masters, looming out of the darkness on the stairs above him.

"I'd be glad," said Egerton, "though it's early."

"Ready in a minute, sir," said Masters, slipping down, apparently enthusiastic. Egerton saw that he was already dressed.

"Has he been hanging about waiting for me?"

Egerton wondered. " Typical of the chap. Regular nurse-maid." He smiled.

Coming back to the library where the fire was being skilfully coaxed into temporary warmth by the attendant Masters, he found the little writing pad lying on top of the voluminous documents. He picked it up. It read : " Five grains. A cold, bitter morning. What sort of accident ? "

He turned to take his tea. "I wonder no one spotted that cold morning," he thought. " That's very interesting."

II

The landlord at the Fox and Duck, the better of the two inns at Aston Pleasant, was unfeignedly delighted to welcome a visitor. The summer had been too dry for any but the most enthusiastic fishermen and they had gone away disappointed ; but now the rain had set in and there was a chance of sport, and when he saw the tall, fair-headed man, with his waterproof case of rods, he came out in person to show him his rooms. Egerton asked if there was a private sitting-room available, and was allotted one with a speckled stuffed trout in a glass case over the mantelpiece, a print of "Blowing Bubbles " and a whisky advertisement on the walls, and a row of books by Edgar Wallace and Earl Der Biggers ranged along the sideboard, these last in case the hurricane that was threatening might defeat even his enthusiasm and he be driven, in despair, to reading.

" I expect you're glad for the rain," Egerton

remarked conversationally, after acknowledging the pretensions of the library. " This place must have been strange with none of its falls running. They're the main feature of the landscape to my way of thinking."

" Folks don't worry about landscape the way they did," the landlord informed him mournfully. " They're all for what's comfortable and convenient now. I had an Irish clergyman and his wife here this summer, and they said thank heaven it's kept dry. You can step over the falls practically everywhere and save yourself miles of walking."

" Why don't such people go to Richmond Park ? " wondered Egerton aloud. " Still there ought to be some fish rising now."

Next morning, however, he left his rods at home and went down to the office of the local paper. He said he wanted to look up the details of an accident that had taken place at Woden Cross on the 26th October.

" What was the name ? " asked the man in the office.

" I don't remember. But there can't have been a great many fatal accidents in this neighbourhood on that particular day. It was quite early in the morning."

" So it 'ud be in the issue of the 28th ? We publish of a Friday."

" There ought to be a note about the inquest, too."

As Egerton had surmised, there was not much choice of accidents ; an elderly woman had been burnt to death while cleaning gloves with petrol on the evening of the 23rd, and a lad had been found in a by-lane, fatally injured, with his motor-cycle, on the morning of the 26th.

"That's probably the one I'm looking for," remarked Egerton. "Lucas. Will the account of the inquest be in this paper?"

"Yes, they held the inquest the next afternoon. I remember about that. It 'ud just get in."

"Was there anything special about it?" Egerton asked, looking up from the newspaper file.

"The young fellow was the son of a pretty influential man here. This motor-cycle was a new sort of toy to him, you see. He hadn't had it above a few months; used to scorch a bit, of course, like the other lads. His father was always warning him that one day he'd break his neck, but he laughed, the way these young chaps do. Well, one evening he was going over to Aston Lacey, matter of thirty miles, I suppose, with some other young chaps, and he telephoned to his father that he might be staying the night. So when he didn't turn up no one worried about him, and they locked up the house and went to bed. The next morning his father went out early—he used to walk the dog about seven or earlier all through the summer and autumn, all the year, in fact, except those bitter dark mornings when only a lunatic goes out for fun—and at the turn of the lane he found his lad with the motor bicycle on top of him. Just about breathing the boy was, and that's all. The old man lifted the machine bodily off him and looked to see what was wrong. It was a rotten sort of smash. He wasn't a doctor, but he could see the boy was pretty bad. Ribs broken and one of the arms, and the right leg just a pulp. He couldn't lift him, and there wasn't any one he could get hold of. There was an A.A. telephone a quarter of a mile away and he ran to that and rang up Dr. Marshall. 'Come hell-for-leather,' he said. 'I'll be waiting by the boy. And get an ambulance. He's damn bad.' Well, back he went and you know how it is when you're waiting—every minute seems an hour. And there was the boy unconscious and barely breathing; and no one came down the lane, and the dog began to howl, and it was bitter cold. It had been freezing all night, and the body was heavy with cold. He waited there, he says, the best part of an hour. He could hardly speak for rage when Marshall did get there. He'd been ringing up his house, he told him, and they said he'd left forty minutes ago. He swore he'd have the doctor before the medical authorities for letting a dying boy hang about. Marshall said he'd had to go to a patient who'd died—he'd been as quick as he could. He'd telephoned the ambulance, but there's only one and there'd been some hitch. It didn't arrive till twenty minutes after the doctor. Been out on another job and only just come in. Marshall said afterwards he thought Lucas was going to break a blood-vessel. He made no end of a scene in court, saying he'd have the doctor taken for manslaughter. The boy died, you see, without ever recovering consciousness, about two hours after they got him to the cottage hospital. He must have been lying out there all night, and if he hadn't been a strong young fellow he'd have been dead when his father found him. His friend said they'd wanted him to stop, but he'd decided to come back. It was slippery underfoot, and he was a bit excited—not drunk or anything, you understand, but he was a young chap and fond of life. And he'd said he was going to see what he could knock out of the bike. Said he didn't often have a chance of a clear road. Well, he knocked hell out of her and out of himself too. The inquiry showed that there wouldn't have been a chance for him, not if he'd been found the minute after he crashed. He knocked himself to pieces inside ; must have had a pretty dose of pain, they said, before he became unconscious. I thought old Lucas was going mad. It's the only boy, the only child, in fact, and his wife's an invalid, one of the pious snuffling sort, no good to any one. No wonder he'd built everything on that lad. Nice boy, too. Well, he made no end of a scene at the inquest, swore he'd have Marshall struck off the register, but of course he couldn't do anything. The coroner did say that in the circumstances he thought perhaps the doctor should have let the old lady go and come on to the accident, but he didn't even put that very strongly. Every one knew old Mrs. Wolfe might be dying, and he was her regular attendant, you know, so the most you had against him was an error of judgment, and he said, too, he thought the ambulance would have collected the boy straight away, and he'd be getting attention at the Cottage Hospital."

" A nasty dilemma," Egerton agreed. " Has there been any sequel ? "

" Lucas moved out a fortnight afterwards. He'd

retired from business, he was quite a warm man, and he's gone abroad, they say. His wife's in a nursing home again; she kept going in and coming out, and they say she's enjoying it very much. Prostrated at the loss of her only son, you know. Every one walking round her on tiptoe. I daresay she's getting more kick out of life than she's done for years."

"Did Dr. Marshall take it much to heart?"

"He's been looking pretty green lately. And no wonder. It's as if there's a fate against him. This affair, and then all the trouble up at the End House. I'll bet he wishes he hadn't noticed what the old lady died of, and just given a certificate for heart failure. He liked the girl—well, every one did—pretty, too, and here she is waiting to be hanged for murder—I daresay they'll reprieve her, if it comes to that; folk don't like the idea of hanging women—but it doesn't seem to me she gets much change out of that. I'd a long chalk sooner be dead than walled up alive, which is what it amounts to. And then that affair of his sister killing herself——"

"Yes, I'd heard of that. What did she do?"

"Pitched herself out of a window. Oh, she must ha' been mad. She'd always been giddy about heights, though. A bit simple we thought her, but she'd kept the doctor's house for years and as quiet a couple as you could wish to meet. A little bit of a thing, skinny and pert as a hen. Used to spend a lot of her time in the church, always giving windows and such-like. Nothing else to spend her money on, you see."

"Does anybody know why she did it?"

"Said she'd nothing to live for. She'd stopped going to church by that time, and apparently the doctor had said something vague about getting married. So she decided there was nothing for it but to pitch herself out of the window. What I've got against these people," he added thoughtfully, "is the way, when they're upset, they don't think of any one but themselves. She never stopped to think how unpleasant it 'ud be for the chap that came along the pavement and found her there. A dreadful sight she was. Fell on her head, you see, skull all caved in. They put newspapers over the face and so on, and when they took 'em off they said you could read the print on her brains. I know the fellow that found her. It shook him up for days."

Egerton hoped he didn't look as green as he felt; even eighteen months of war on the Western Front hadn't hardened him to the sight of blood and beastliness, and his imagination, that was unusually keen, instantly presented him with a vision of what the pavement must have looked like on that clear summer morning sixteen months ago.

"Have you got the newspaper reports on that file?" he asked, steeling his nerves to go through with the hideous affair.

"Not on that file. But I could get 'em for you. You'll have to pay a fee."

Egerton jerked half a crown on to the counter. He hoped this loquacious fellow would find something to do while he himself went through the reports, though perhaps his aversion to the man was both illogical and ungenerous considering that he really had told him a great deal of what he wanted to know.

Luck stood in with him now; some one else needed attention, and Egerton found himself alone with the file of last year's papers before him, and both leisure and solitude in which to examine them.

SHOCKING WINDOW FALL TRAGEDY
INQUEST ON MISS EMMA MARSHALL
BROTHER'S EVIDENCE

At Aston Pleasant on Wednesday last, the 15th July, the inquest was held on Miss Emma Marshall, sister of Dr. Marshall, the well-known physician and surgeon. Miss Marshall died of injuries received in falling from a first-floor window on the early morning of the 14th; death must have been practically instantaneous. According to the evidence, it is supposed that Miss Marshall fell from her window at about five a.m., an hour when the street would be quite empty. The body was found by Herbert Packer, a labourer on his way to work. The skull had struck the pavement and was terribly fractured. There was blood all over the stones and on the dead lady's nightgown.

Dr. Marshall, who gave evidence of identification, said that his sister had always been afraid of heights, and would not willingly linger near a window, even so near the ground as the first-floor. All her friends knew of this idiosyncrasy, which made it the more strange that she should meet her death in this fashion. On the other hand, had she intended to take her life, it was probable that this method would be the first to occur to her. In reply to a queston by the coroner, he said that he should hesitate to call her neurotic ; she was perhaps impulsive, capable of great enthusiasm that she would squeeze into one channel. Thus, as the village people knew, there had been a time when all her interests had been religious ones. She spent a great part of her day in the church, and gave generously to all the collections, as well as frequent donations to its embellishment. During the past few months she had retired from almost all her parochial activities. He had once or twice suggested the unwisdom of this violent break, but she had been so unusually resentful of his advice that he had not proffered it again.

" Had she, in the parlance of the day, lost faith, Dr. Marshall ? "

" I think that is the way it's generally put. She said, ' I've discovered now what you might have told me years ago, that there's no God. I've been decking a heathen temple. But that's the last they'll ever see of my money.' "

" Did it upset her, this sudden change in beliefs ? "

" She attached herself rigidly to new interests. She spent a great deal of time at the End House, becoming a fast friend of Mrs. Wolfe."

" You perhaps objected to this friendship ? "

" Objected is rather a strong word. I knew my sister's temperament very well, and I had only the normal man's desire that she shouldn't, to use another colloquialism, put all her eggs into one basket."

"Do you suggest, Dr. Marshall, that it was Mrs. Wolfe's influence that weaned your sister from her religious beliefs?"

"I think it's no secret to say that Mrs. Wolfe is a freethinker. She proclaims it herself on every possible occasion."

"And she persuaded your sister to adopt her views."

"That is my impression."

"You yourself never tried to argue such matters with Miss Marshall?"

"No. I knew that her nature must cling desperately to something, and she wasn't extravagant as doctors understand the term, in her religion. She didn't try and starve herself or anything of that kind, as religious ladies frequently do. She was content to live normally and find her pleasure in her ecclesiastical interests. And though I didn't share them, we never had a disagreement on the subject."

"Had your sister seemed at all strange, distraite, lately?"

"I think she felt the loss of her faith. But she was comparatively normal. I can't mention any special incident that disquieted me."

"And on the day before she died, did you see much of her?"

"Yes. We had lunch together and I asked her what she was doing in the afternoon. She said she was going out to tea with a lady who lived near by. As a matter of fact, she was getting ready to start when I left the house on a rather long round of visits."

"Did her manner at that meal strike you as being in any way unusual ?"

"I can't say it did. We talked, as always, just local chit-chat ; she told me about a gas fire that wanted seeing to—you know the kind of thing. Presently I happened to say I'd been visiting a married friend of mine, a new-made Benedict, and it made one realise what one had missed. She asked me if I were thinking of getting married, and I replied that at present I was wedded to my practice, but that didn't mean I'd put the idea finally out of my mind. A country doctor's living in these hard times doesn't give him much margin for luxuries."

"Did your sister seem at all distressed at the idea ?"

"That didn't strike me at the time, but, thinking it over afterwards, I seem to remember that she was unduly anxious. I remember chaffing her and saying, 'Well, I'm not going to be married next week. Cheer up.' As a matter of fact, I am not even engaged to be married. I was half-joking with her, and I certainly had no idea that she might take my suggestion so seriously as to imagine that she would be unwanted or without a home. I had much too strong a sense of what I owed her, for keeping my home so well in the past and for all her consideration. She was a wealthy woman and she had helped me a good deal in my younger days. We'd always been thrown together a lot ; you couldn't call her an invalid, but on the other hand her health was not robust. I don't think she could have stood a life of great excitement or energy."

"But you do think now that perhaps she brooded

on what you had said half in jest, and that that contributed to her view that there was no place for her anywhere ? "

" I reproach myself most bitterly for the suggestion, particularly as it had no foundation. Had I really been contemplating marriage, I should, of course, have discussed the position with her, and seen what arrangement we could make. I should certainly never have suggested her leaving the village where she had all her friends and interests."

" You said just now, Dr. Marshall, that she was an impulsive woman. If she got the idea into her head that she was superfluous, she might carry out her dreadful plan without giving the position true consideration."

" That is quite likely."

" And in the evening, when you returned, did she seem at all strange in her manner ? "

" No, except that she asked for wine for dinner, a thing she never did. But I didn't think much of it at the time. One has these sudden fancies. And otherwise, she seemed perfectly normal."

Mrs. Wolfe in her evidence said that Miss Marshall had been a friend of hers for several months ; previous to that they had been acquaintances, meeting at various local functions. Miss Marshall had been greatly attached to the church when they first met, but after a short time she seemed to transfer her affections. She, Mrs. Wolfe, considered her the type of woman who banks everything on a single enthusiasm. Probably she had first been attracted to the church by the personality of the vicar ; now that spell was beginning to wear thin, and she needed fresh impetus. Mrs. Wolfe assured the court grimly that it had required very little persuasion on her part to separate Miss Marshall from her faith. No, she had never set out to do this, but Miss Marshall had several times asked her for her views on certain points of doctrine and belief. She, Mrs. Wolfe, was a freethinker and believed in nothing. Naturally, when Miss Marshall asked her, she told her so. When Miss Marshall asked for reasons she had produced them. Of course she had set up her sturdy atheism against Miss Marshall's pallid Christianity ; it was not, she considered, her fault if the orthodoxy of the one had been easily vanquished by the whole-hearted disbelief of the other. She had never urged Miss Marshall to abandon her religion, nor had she ever jeered at her practices. Some people, she knew, needed crutches, and Miss Marshall had no other interests. When Miss Marshall told her that she was giving up her church-going, she had not been hypocritical enough to try to persuade her to change her mind. She would not say that she had noticed any hysterical tendency in Miss Marshall, though she was inclined to get very much excited over trifles. She never heard her complain of her brother or his treatment of her, though she did once say that if he should marry she did not know what she should do.

"Was that recently ?"

"No, some weeks ago. And the question was never raised again."

"When did you last see Miss Marshall ?"

"On Monday. She came over to tea. She seemed

very cheerful and certainly didn't give one any idea that there was anything wrong."

"And when you heard what had happened?"

"On the morning in question I had a letter from her, a very wild note with no beginning and no proper ending. It just said: 'I have lost God, so there is nothing for me hereafter; and Harry tells me I am to lose him, so there is no hope for me here. There is nothing left.—Emma.'" (This letter in Miss Marshall's big characteristic handwriting was handed to the jury and was afterwards photographed by an enterprising reporter and reproduced in the press. Egerton saw a photograph of it in the *Grebeshire News*, and another, a vastly better specimen, in the *Morning Record*, on his return to town.)

"That arrived on the morning of the 15th?"

"Yes. I am not on the telephone, so I could not ring up and ask for news, but I sent my daughter to the post office with a guarded message. I simply said I should like Miss Marshall to come to lunch with me, if she were free."

"And the reply was?"

"That Miss Marshall had met with a serious accident."

"Did you ascertain how serious?"

"It was my daughter at the telephone, not myself. She elicited no details."

"And when did you hear the facts?"

"After breakfast I went over to Aston Pleasant by omnibus. I was anxious, and I did not care to start rumours by telephoning. I went straight to Miss Marshall's house, and was told that she was not there. I said I would wait for the doctor to come back, as every one seemed very mysterious. He came in about half an hour later and I showed him the letter. He was very badly upset and kept saying, 'So she did it on purpose; she did it on purpose; she must have been mad.' I said crisply that in my opinion any one who walked out of a window in a nightdress was mad. Then he looked at the letter again, and said, 'What does she mean, she is to lose me?' I said he must know better than I did, and he thought, and then he said, 'She can't have meant because I joked about being married. But she seemed all right in the afternoon. It can't have been that.'"

"But you thought it was that?"

"I didn't see what else it could be. She was very impulsive and apt to act on the spur of the minute."

Mrs. Barclay, with whom Miss Marshall was to have spent the afternoon of the 14th, said that at the eleventh hour she had telephoned Miss Marshall, putting her off, as she had had a sudden domestic upset, and her maid was leaving at an hour's notice. In the circumstances she did not feel up to receiving visitors. She was sure Miss Marshall would understand.

Miss Ethel Morrison said that she had called by chance at Miss Marshall's house that afternoon in the hopes of finding her at home. Miss Marshall had come down in her best frock and had told her that she had just had a telephone call from Mrs. Barclay postponing the tea-party. She had begged Miss Morrison to stay and spend the afternoon with her as she would be alone, even the servant having gone out. After tea Miss Marshall had said suddenly, " Have you ever thought of my brother as a marrying man ? " Miss Morrison had laughed and said, " Well, you know what they say. No fool like an old fool. And of course he's very handsome." Miss Marshall said, " Do they talk much about it in the village ? " Miss Morrison said she didn't think so ; she never heard it. But, of course, a bachelor always came in for a certain amount of chaff. Miss Marshall had pressed her to know if any special name was being mentioned, and she had reluctantly admitted that some people had wondered—but very discreetly, she was sure—if the doctor wasn't rather taken by Miss —— But nothing more definite than that. She, witness, thought Miss Marshall looked rather depressed at the information, so she (witness) had rallied her, saying that after so many years of flawless housekeeping the doctor would think very often before parting with her or exchanging one regime for another. Miss Marshall had said, " Do you think after so many years he would be likely to change his whole way of living ? And even if he did, surely there is room for three of us in this big house ? " Witness admitted unhappily that she had allowed herself to speak seriously on this subject, saying that in her opinion such an arrangement was never a success. She had not realised that Miss Marshall was really worrying over the position, or not more than any woman with an attractive unmarried brother must occasionally. She had not herself taken the position seriously, and she would have been as surprised as any one else if the doctor had announced his engagement in the course of the next few days. She had stayed with Miss Marshall until about seven o'clock ; the doctor had not then returned, and Miss Marshall had said with a sort of laugh that perhaps he was with Miss —— at that very minute.

Miss —— said furiously that she had never heard this despicable piece of gossip before, that the doctor was old enough to be her father, and that anyway she was already engaged. She wanted to know if she had a case for defamation of character against the last witness, as her fiancé emphatically wouldn't relish the idea of her name being coupled with Marshall's all round the neighbourhood. She hadn't met the doctor half a dozen times, and he certainly didn't give her the idea of a man to get maudlin over a young woman.

That, with some testimonies by the servants and by the vicar, who had deplored Miss Marshall's break with her faith, and had on several occasions endeavoured to restore her to the fold, but without success, closed the inquest, and the verdict was Suicide while of Unsound Mind.

" And to think," was Egerton's comment, " that that old woman was the only one to see the gigantic flaw in the whole scheme. Though it might have occurred to various other people that it isn't exactly acting on impulse to post a letter announcing your intention at six o'clock—I see the last post goes out from here at six—and wait nearly twelve hours to carry it out. No wonder the old lady was pleased with herself. She'd got this man under her thumb, and she could do what she liked with him. I bet she kept that letter as proof, and she could always back it up by producing the printed version of the inquest. Power. Marshall himself said that was what she lived for. And she meant to use it. I'll swear all I've got that she wasn't going to let him marry that girl, and probably by this time, a man of his age and temperament, he was crazy for her. He'd never know a safe minute while Mrs. Wolfe lived. He had to get rid of her, but, by Jove, what a chance he took. Just as he took a chance when he murdered his sister. I wonder if he drugged her first. I shouldn't be surprised. And he had nothing against him but sheer ill-luck. That accident—and Mrs. Barclay's quarrel with her maid. Ridiculous trifles to wreck a man's plans and eventually to bring him to the scaffold. Because his head's securely in the noose now, and unless he can manage to take an easier way out, it'll hang him. And now I'd better go back and report to my youthful clients."

He didn't see Dr. Marshall. He didn't want to. He knew he was a tall muscular man, handsome and popular. That was all he needed to know.

CHAPTER IX

I

EGERTON had telegraphed to Anthony, and as his train drew in at King's Cross he saw that conspicuous smooth red head moving in the crowd. Anthony came across and took his case.

"Let me. We can get a taxi outside. I've got in

touch with the others, and they're all waiting for you at my cousin, Norman Bell's, rooms. I hope you feel up to going through with it to-night." But his manner expressed no shadow of doubt. Whether Egerton felt like it or not, he had no choice.

It was already nearly nine o'clock; London was dark with brilliant points of light in windows and doors, and round golden globes, where lamp-posts reared their heads by the kerb. Gleams of red and green betrayed the whereabouts of traffic signals, and in spite of the rain that had been falling for the past hour the streets were full of people. Scarlet omnibuses came rushing past, crowded chiefly with women; couples strolled on the pavement; men with coat-collars turned up shoved their hands in their pockets and audibly cursed the bloody rain; the lights were up in many of the windows in the Tottenham Court Road, and as they approached Oxford Street, more of the night-life of London was evident. The theatres were full, but people emerging from restaurants moved languidly along the pavements; taxis went past, sometimes with solitary men bowling along to some appointment, more often with a couple, smiling, eager, or inwardly withdrawn. You could only see their faces as the light from the street lamps caught them for an instant, before they were inexorably borne away into obscurity. The river, thought Anthony, would be a black tide, surging with a dark oily smoothness; there might be boats about, but they would only be discernible by the little points of light they displayed; and the surface would be splintered with silver where the rain broke up its smoothness with a thousand gleaming lances.

Egerton, he thought, in a glimpse he had during a momentary traffic hold-up, was looking worn; there was a pallor about him that wasn't his normal pallor of health, and for the first time Anthony began to realise the magnitude of the responsibility he and Rose had casually fastened to shoulders already burdened with two men's work. He began to feel a little uncomfortable, to wonder if he should speak, but before he could do that Egerton said thoughtfully, "It's odd how one never seems wholly alive out of London. Other towns have their individuality to which, I suppose, one makes some kind of more or less adequate response, but one's conscious of waiting to release the whole volume till one's home."

Anthony said eagerly, "It's like that with me, too. Oh, those nights on tour when you can't sleep and you wonder if you'll ever be off the road. I remember a night at some fourth-rate little town in the Midlands; the last lodger had left souvenirs in the bed and I got up and sat on the window-sill. It was a queer sort of night with clouds blowing across the moon, and there wasn't a soul stirring. And suddenly all the clocks on earth began to chime. It was eerie for a minute, and then I remembered—*I have heard the bells at midnight, Master Shallow.* And I thought of a night when my luck was out and I'd stood under Big Ben and heard it strike midnight and another when it was in and I got up and went to see the carts arriving at Covent Garden, and presently heard St. Paul's chime six."

Egerton said, with apparent irrelevance, " I liked that show of yours at the Royal. What are you doing now ? "

" Looking for a job," confessed Anthony. " What's known as resting, though Heaven is my witness there's precious little rest about it. I should think dockers are about the only people who get up as early as we do looking for non-existent worms."

" What about that play Burminster is putting on at the New Westminster ? "

" Not a chance, apparently. I've had a shot."

Egerton took a card from his pocket, and scribbled a line on it.

" Go and see Burminster in the morning. I'll ring him up early and tell him to expect you. I think you're the sort that might suit him. Not that I can promise anything, of course."

" Of course not," agreed Anthony mechanically, looking at the card. For the moment his exultation was so great that he forgot about Carol, about Derek, and the meaning of this companionship in the taxi to-night. Egerton, glancing at him sideways, thought, He'll do, and the old familiar excitement that contact with humanity kindled in him shot up, burning away his weariness and apprehension. Because he knew that the case he was going to put to them a few minutes hence was far from complete, and he couldn't in the least see how they were going to perfect it.

Norman had got drinks ready and a plate of sandwiches, in case Egerton hadn't dined, but Egerton explained that he had had dinner on the train. Anthony introduced Norman, suave and composed as always, holding in his emotion with an iron restraint; Neville, watchful and anxious, and as sick as hell about Derek. Rose, Egerton had met already. Then they all sat down. No one had thanked Egerton for throwing up his job or for coming at this late hour to a stranger's house; their need for all he could do for them had gone too far for such conventionalities.

Egerton plunged straight into the story. "The case isn't by any means finished," he warned them. "I can only give you the bare bones. I'd better tell you what I think happened, and then you'll have to take the next step." His rare smile flashed at them. "What I've got for you is simply a collection of facts; the difficult part of the job I'm leaving to you. I begin about six months ago, on the day before Miss Marshall met her death. You'll remember that she was a comparatively wealthy woman keeping house for her brother, who was a by no means wealthy man; and a man, I think, of reckless tastes. On his admission she'd helped him financially more than once; I don't know whether they called these transactions loans, but in the light of what happened, I think that very probable. They lived simply, because Miss Marshall wasn't the type who can understand extravagance or even luxury; she wasn't mean, I think, or consciously cheeseparing, but she simply didn't want any other way of life. She had a definite position; a doctor in a small community, particularly when he's a bachelor, is quite a personage. That position had obtained for several years. Miss Marshall was pretty well satisfied; she did a good deal of church work and presumably went about as much as she wanted. I'm not sure she wasn't the type who thinks it sinful to be comfortable. But the doctor had other views. They say he was beginning to talk of marriage; he may have wanted a more intimate domesticity than his sister made possible; there may have been some particular woman. If so, her name (I feel sure) hasn't been mentioned. The point is, he was sick and tired of the present regime. The servants had been in the family for years, they wouldn't talk. The odds are that there were disagreements; the doctor felt hampered. It's galling to a man of his temperament to live with a rich woman, who doesn't care about spending what she has. Anyhow, he wanted to get married and he could not afford it. I dare say there were debts; admittedly he was a bit of a gambler. And he decided he must have her money and get her out of the way. He's cool-headed; the way he turned the case against your cousin proves that. He laid his plans some time ahead; it was a valuable card in his hand that his sister should lose faith, and turn all her attention to Mrs. Wolfe. It made suicide so much more probable; people might have found it difficult to believe she would take her life, considering her religious reputation. And there was never any question of mania. So he laid a very subtle and simple suicide plan. Miss Marshall's writing is large and not difficult to copy; Marshall wrote a letter to Mrs. Wolfe, signed with his sister's name, saying she was taking her life as she'd nothing left to live for. He sowed the seed during lunch, speaking of being married, of fresh domestic arrangements. I expect Miss Marshall was upset; she probably had enough sense to realise that her position, even with her money, as an unattached elderly lady, wouldn't compare with her position as her brother's hostess. She may even have said she wanted her money back, the money she had lent him. There are no witnesses of that conversation; the jury had to take the doctor's word for everything. It appears that that afternoon Miss Marshall was going out; her brother hung about until she actually went upstairs to get ready. The post went at six o'clock; he took the letter with him when he left the house, dropped it into the box and went on his rounds. What he couldn't foresee was that at three forty-five a telephone message would come through putting Miss Marshall off. The servant was out that afternoon, and about three-fifty a friend arrived, who stayed talking to Miss Marshall until after seven. I don't know whether the doctor knew that when he came back; if he did he must have realised his danger. If any one questioned the time that the letter was posted, it would be obvious that Miss Marshall couldn't have posted it, because she'd been indoors, and there was a witness to prove this, between half-past twelve, when the first post went, and half-past six or after, when it would be too late for letters posted that night to be delivered next morning; and the servant had gone out directly after lunch, so she couldn't have taken it; and in any case she didn't. I've ascertained that. However, he had to go on now. Mrs. Wolfe would get the letter in the morning and would probably come over or send a message at once, and Marshall couldn't risk any one knowing that his sister hadn't writter the note at all. He *had* to go on and trust to blind chance that no one saw the discrepancy. According to the evidence, Miss Marshall asked for wine that night; she was unused to it, and it's quite possible that the doctor administered some drug. People who don't drink wine often are apt to dislike the taste, and she wouldn't notice the addition. I think something like that must have happened from the description of the body when found. I've seen the doctor's house; the rooms are low, and if one fell from an upper window, particularly a woman as light and small as Miss Marshall, I doubt if the skull would be crushed as it was. It seems to me she was flung down, with force, with violence. If she were in a drugged sleep that would be simple; Marshall's a big powerful man."

Rose drew a shuddering breath. Anthony laid a hand gently on hers. "Brace up!" he muttered.

Neville said in inscrutable tones, "And the question of the letter was never raised at the verdict?"

"Apparently not. The only person who seems to have realised its importance was Mrs. Wolfe. I think that must be so, because Marshall can have had no motive for her murder unless she had him in her power. He wasn't gaining anything materially by her death, she wasn't a burden on him, he could even have refused to attend her. But instead of that he put her out of the way, with diabolical cunning; so she must have recognised the weapon that letter was to her. She held it over his head; I'm convinced of that. She would love the position. Marshall himself told the jury at her inquest that she was a woman to whom power was an obsession, and he spoke from personal knowledge. She was the fiercer, I dare say, because she couldn't really dominate any of you. That's galling to a woman of her nature. But the doctor she had got, and meant to keep. She wasn't going to let him marry, and she wasn't going to let him forget she held his life in her hands. He had his sister's money, but she'd see to it it was remarkably little use to him. He'd been better off during Miss Marshall's lifetime. And so for him there was really no alternative ; he had to put Mrs. Wolfe out of the way. Then she had this attack ; it was a matter of patience, of course, for sooner or later he must have known she'd have some such crisis ; and then the morphia came into play. For a day there was a chance she was going to die ; he must have been on tenterhooks then, not knowing whether she'd left any information in writing behind her, confided in any one. Then she got better ; she wouldn't die so long as she had some one to torment. And he laid his plans. He knew the ordering of the house, that she had invalid food at a certain hour each night. That was his chance. He came late, so that the tray would be in place ; but he knew she wouldn't have had it before his arrival. He was lucky in that she insisted on seeing him alone ; probably she guessed where he'd spent the evening and wanted to torment him about it. There's a note among the papers you gave me of Mrs. Wolfe saying some one shouldn't get married on her forty thousand pounds. You all took it to mean the forty thousand she had left her favourite grandchild, but it's an odd coincidence that Marshall benefited by precisely the same sum by his sister's death. And it seems to me much more probable that it was that forty thousand to which Mrs. Wolfe referred. She doesn't seem to have paid much attention to the risk she herself ran by having him as her doctor, but probably she thought herself amply guarded. I am sure she would never have allowed him to give her an injection. She could hardly fail to realise that he was dangerous to her. A man who has not stuck at one wilful murder is not very likely to be very squeamish about another. As it was, he dropped the morphia in to the invalid food on his way out. He had a certain recklessness that wasn't afraid of taking heavy odds. He wrote that letter and posted it to Mrs. Wolfe before he took the first step towards murdering his sister; something might have occurred to prevent him, but he took the hazard. And here he put the poison into the cup and went home. The next step had to wait till morning. Another thing he couldn't have foreseen was the accident to that boy. He was summoned at ten minutes to seven; he was dressed, I think, waiting to be called to the End House. He mustn't be out, in case another doctor was called in, or in case Dr. Bell himself took charge in the emergency; on the other hand, it would arouse suspicion and bring him into disfavour if he neglected the boy. It must have been a frightful choice for him, but eventually he chanced his reputation and merely telephoned the ambulance. He counted, I suppose, on no one noticing the precise moment of the two calls; he could represent them as having come much closer together than actually they did. As soon as you rang up he came over hell-for-leather; another man might have given the certificate for heart trouble or sudden collapse, but he wasn't taking any chances; the thing was going to be settled definitely once and for all. He asked for the morphia and then he got the room to himself; he sent you, Dr. Bell, on some errand, and then got Miss John to follow after you. During the minute or two you were away he emptied the morphia phial, refilled it with water, and waited for you to come back. He was going to make the horrifying discovery in the presence of as many witnesses as possible. The second thing he had failed to allow for was that the windows would be so stiff they would stick; that explains the open window mentioned in the evidence. That struck me as a grave discrepancy; of course, he hadn't much time, and once again he had to trust that no one would notice. But it was taking a long chance, when you remember that some one had spoken of the room smelling of rum, which it wouldn't have done if the window had been open all night; and Miss Carol shivered because there was a cold blast of air. Who opened that window? and why? It wasn't open at seven o'clock before the doctor came, and it was open at eight, when he'd been alone in the room for three minutes. And I was puzzled too, to know why he should supply your cousin with five grains of morphia, when he was visiting daily, and she was giving injections of a quarter of a grain. Morphia isn't a thing one's casual about. He had, I argued, some purpose in giving her that quantity. Well, there's your story. Now you've got to find the proof."

II

Egerton had gone as soon as he'd finished talking, and Rose went with him—Anthony saw them out. When he came back he found Neville and Norman staring at one another, both rather shaken.

" Game and rubber to Rose," observed Anthony cheerfully. " I must say Derek's a lucky devil. The two nicest women I know in love with him. Oh, there's no secret about Rose, though, in spite of everything, I still have hopes. She isn't the kind to stand still and emulate Lot's wife when there's so much ahead."

" God knows how we're going to meet Derek after this," said Norman wretchedly.

" You didn't make the evidence," Anthony pointed out, reasonably. " It's like a jigsaw puzzle, a test of your skill. I must say," he added, in a more sober voice, " that chap Egerton's pretty bright. He only had the same facts to work on, as we did, but he got there and we came the most frightful cropper. Still, we might have known it wasn't Derek. These imaginative beggars never do any of the amazing things they write about. They have to keep it for their works, I suppose. Well, well, we seem to have done all we can for the moment."

" Are you suggesting we shall leave things as they are ? " said Neville drily.

" No, I think this is Aunt Dorothy's cue. Bless the girl, what should we do without her ? "

III

Since her mother's funeral Dorothy John had scarcely been seen in the village. Rumour said she was going round the house tearing up every old photograph and every scrap of paper connected with her former life, and opinion was divided between those who thought this violence unnecessarily dramatic and ill-suited to a lady of her suppressed tastes, and those who lauded such affection for a parent who, say what you like, must often have seemed a blend of whips and scorpions. But one day—it was thirty-six hours after Egerton's departure from Norman Bell's rooms—she put on her top-heavy black velvet hat, her black coat with its oppressive black fur collar, drew on black kid gloves, took a black handbag and a black umbrella and went into the village. One or two people who met her and whose faces immediately assumed a discreet expression of grief, were amazed to see her cheerful smile and hear her light-hearted greeting. "Such a lovely morning," she said inaccurately, waggling her unseaworthy umbrella at an acquaintance. "So pleasant after the heat."

She went first to the chemist, where she produced the kind of list you might expect, a strip of blue linen notepaper torn off some one's letter and hoarded for thrift's sake.

"A bottle of Eno's fruit salts," she said, "and a hot-water bottle. Oh, good morning, Mr. Whirter. Isn't this rain refreshing? Yes, most pleasant, I'm sure."

"It's nice to see you about again, miss," said Mr. Whirter formally.

Dorothy beamed. "Yes. I haven't liked to come out before, with all the trouble we've been having. Poor mama's death and then this scandal about my niece. But now all that's cleared up so satisfactorily, well, there really doesn't seem any point staying at home behind the blinds, does there? Like that man in the Bible who washed his face and came out of his room—I forget why, but it made him happy."

"Cleared up, miss?" murmured Mr. Whirter, respectfully holding on to the bottle of salts, and not seeing that black kid-gloved hand outstretched for its owner's parcel. "I'm glad, I'm sure, but I didn't know . . ."

"But nor did I until yesterday. One of my nephews explained it to me. It's all rather confusing if you haven't got a legal mind, but it seems it's quite clear that Dr. Marshall did it himself. Oh, yes, he did. I can't tell you how they worked that out, but they explained to me, and I saw it then perfectly. It's such splendid news, isn't it?"

"Dr. Marshall?" repeated Mr. Whirter dazedly.

"Yes. It appears he murdered his sister, too, and my mother found out about it, and made things rather uncomfortable for him. Just what mama would have done, of course. Find out, I mean."

The chemist was staring, open-mouthed. "Miss John, you know—you know that's libel. The doctor could have you in court—I mean, it's very dangerous."

"It's very dangerous throwing people out of

windows," said Dorothy serenely, possessing herself of the salts and making a triumphant exit.

In the draper's she ran against Hilary Musgrave. She smiled and touched her elbow and said, "I'm so sorry." Hilary turned round and stared at her.

"She's getting odd," she thought, crossing the street. "Well, that kind of life was enough to make her." She was choosing electric fittings for her new home, and the thought of Dorothy John didn't detain her more than a few seconds.

In the draper's Dorothy found herself alongside Mrs. Mead, the acknowledged gossip of the town.

"That poor girl," Dorothy observed cheerfully, ordering white sarsenet ribbon.

"Which girl?"

"Miss Musgrave. A dreadful thing to happen, and apt to blight one's chances later."

"What's a dreadful thing to happen?"

"About the doctor, I mean."

"The doctor?" Mrs. Mead thrilled and her face lighted up. "My dear, what's that?"

"Well, of course she won't be able to marry him now. That's what mama felt."

"Do you mean to say there's something wrong with the doctor?"

"Well, I don't know about wrong. But I can't help agreeing with mama that he oughtn't to marry that girl without telling her."

"Telling her what?"

"The truth."

"About . . .?"

"His sister—and mama, too, I suppose. But, of course, that would be dreadfully risky. She might have one of those inconvenient consciences and thing he ought to give himself up. That was why she wouldn't let them marry before. I suppose if she had he wouldn't have killed her."

"The doctor wouldn't have killed your mother?" Stark incomprehension informed Mrs. Mead's ferrety little face.

"Yes. He did, you know. Oh, yes, there's no secret about it any more. It's all coming out. We're waiting till the trial. It won't be long now. And dear Carol quite understands that's for the best. Such clever fellows, my nephews, as that nice red-headed one once said to me. It's a pity grandmother doesn't appreciate us, he said, because we are a clever lot. And, you know, I think they are. I'm sure I could never have discovered about the doctor. But it's all quite certain now. So odd, somehow, to think of his coming in and out of the house and all the time a murderer."

She paid fourpence for her ribbon, took pins instead of the odd farthing and disappeared.

"What do you make of that?" Mrs. Mead asked the girl behind the counter. "Is she crazy or—— You know, I've often thought there was something sinister about Dr. Marshall, and of course it was queer his sister dying like that and leaving him all the money."

Round the village of Aston Merry the rumour spread, the astonishing, the incredible, the desperately exciting rumour that Dr. Marshall had coolly murdered two women and was prepared to see a third die without lifting a finger to save her. Soon the story was all over Aston Pleasant, too. The doctor was aware of strange glances. Hilary Musgrave came to him presently demanding, "Have you heard what they're saying about you, Harry?"

"What's that?"

"That you killed Mrs. Wolfe."

"My dear, every man has his enemies. If it weren't that they'd find I was a secret drug-taker or drank myself blind every night."

"I think it's more serious than that. I'm constantly being asked about it, and I don't like it. It's this Miss John. . . ."

"My dear girl, every one knows she's crazy."

"They may think she's crazy, but they listen to what she says."

"Well, I'm not going to give her free advertisement by taking any notice of her maunderings."

"You won't be able to let it go on, Harry. You'll see."

They waited and saw. For the day came when one of the big men in Aston Pleasant cut the doctor dead; other people were calling in the new man who'd set up in the Square; wherever he went Marshall was conscious of strange glances. At last Hilary said frankly: "I don't pay a moment's attention to what they say; it doesn't matter to me, and I don't believe a word of it, but I won't let it ever be whispered by mischief makers that my children have a murderer for their father."

"All right," her lover promised. "I'll talk to a lawyer and see if we can get the poor woman certified."

He went next day to see a man called Clitheroe.

Clitheroe frowned when he heard the story. " What sort of woman is this ? "

" She's Mrs. Wolfe's daughter; she's always been a bit of a half-wit."

" She's not certifiable ? "

" Well, hardly."

" You could bring a libel case against her—or slander, if she hasn't put it into writing."

" That's precisely what she wants, I'm convinced. I know these elderly frustrated women; she's at a bad age, too. What she yearns for is to attract notice at all costs. She's been crushed by that mother of hers all her life."

" All the same, she mustn't be allowed to go round talking like this. You'll soon have people saying that, of course, she was in her mother's confidence, and that's how she knows about your sister's death, and she was in the house at the time of Mrs. Wolfe's. It's too dangerous wholly to disregard, but I don't suppose it'll ever get as far as the court. I'll write to her, as your solicitor, saying we're bringing an action for defamatory libel, and asking for the name of her lawyers. That'll bring her to her senses. If her man's got a grain of intelligence he'll make her publish a refutation of these crazy charges, and you could possibly get damages. There is an estate, isn't there ? "

But Dorothy John's reaction to the letter that subsequently reached her was disconcerting. She named Rupert Neville as her solicitor, and said she was prepared to back up her statements in court. She added innocently that anyway they'd be public property so soon as the trial started. Neville didn't appear to be putting any reasonable restraint on her extravagances, merely intimating his willingness to appear for his client when the case was called.

Clitheroe was uneasy.

" They've got something up their sleeve," he told the doctor. " This is a bad bit of business for you, Harry. A doctor's position is always a delicate one, and if a divorce action can make him rock, a murder hint generally brings him toppling. I think we'd better settle this out of court, at any cost, if it can be managed."

But it seemed as though it couldn't. Every day more people were, in Dorothy John's phrase, too busy thinking of the pretty angels when the doctor approached to recognise him ; and presently he took the settlement into his own hands in the only way that was left to him. Sentimentalists said he was a sportsman really, backing big odds and losing. But Neville remarked in vigorous tones that he was more like a defaulting bookie, who ran away because he was afraid to pay up. But he had to admit that the letter he left behind for the coroner counted a good many points in his favour.

" I should hate to cost the country five thousand pounds, particularly at a time when money is scarce and thrills are cheap. Moreover, I prefer to be remembered by the profession that I have followed for thirty years, rather than by the adventitious character I was compelled to assume on two occasions. My only point is that I consider the legal system wants tightening up ; you, sir, have presided at two scenes of murder in which I personally have been involved ; and on each occasion you have been completely out in your reckonings and unimaginative—I might almost say unenterprising—in your conclusions. Incidentally, it has taken a woman—and I have always despised women—to give my career this abrupt closing. It may be thought that I should admire them—women, I mean—for their perspicacity so far as I am concerned, but as a logical being I do nothing of the kind. Only with Adam do I cry, Behold this woman, God's second thought—and how seldom are second thoughts profitable."

EPILOGUE

"I WONDER what it is about weddings that makes them such exhausting affairs," Anthony remarked to his youngest cousin as they left the church where Derek and Carol had just been made man and wife.

"You're so unimportant at a wedding," Rose pointed out. "That's rather galling for you, isn't it?"

"The new psychology. Perhaps you're right. And yet I swear I could enjoy my own, given certain circumstances."

Rose said calmly, "Damn this rain. How nice the south of France must be. Those lucky devils."

"Well, I don't envy 'em. And I couldn't go to France now anyhow. We're rehearsing," for Egerton's introduction had obtained for him the chance he had been out for, though no amount of introductions would have persuaded Burminster even to try him if he'd not been impressed by the vigour, charm and talent of his applicant. " Besides, every one out there is so refined these days. I'd be like a fish out of water. So would you; you'd go snooping round after life-stories for your serials. Not because you'd want to, but because you couldn't help yourself. I know."

" You know a lot," Rose agreed, with unimpaired cheerfulness.

" I know what I want, anyhow."

" A lot of us do that."

" No, we only think we know."

Rose bit her lip. She'd wondered how she'd get through this business of seeing Derek married to some one else; on the whole, it was less dreadful than she'd expected.

" Let's go in there," suggested Anthony, indicating a large flaring white building, covered with the names of film stars, and gaudy with photographs. " That's my favourite girl. I adore her."

They sat at the back of the hall; the warmth and darkness, the sense of intimacy that such circumstances engender, Anthony's soft chuckle, his touch on Rose's elbow at a critical moment, his gaiety that nothing could quench, rekindled the flame that for weeks now had burnt so low. After all, thought Rose, life can't be over at twenty-two. It was a consoling reflection.

The big picture ended; Mickey Mouse came on. Anthony murmured that he was probably the biggest peace-maker since Edward VII. You couldn't remain stiff or at enmity while he shot up trees, balanced precariously on twigs, fell through space, splashed into rivers, was chased by alligators, pulled himself out by a giant rhubarb plant growing on the bank, somersaulted into a wall to escape a neighbouring dog, saw stars, rolled back into the water. . . .

Rose laughed aloud; her laughter chimed with Anthony's.

" Fun," he said in his warm caressing voice.

" Yes," agreed Rose, reflecting with some surprise that anything done with Anthony always was. And then, much more unexpectedly, " I wonder if, years ahead, I'll write this up as 'On not marrying your first love.' It is jolly to think that Anthony doesn't object to the commercial mind."

THE END

››› If you've enjoyed this book and would like to discover more great vintage crime and thriller titles, as well as the most exciting crime and thriller authors writing today, visit: ›››

The Murder Room
Where Criminal Minds Meet

themurderroom.com